Jordie in Charge

A Castre World Novel

E. A. SHANNIAK

Eagle Creek Books
Virginia Beach, VA 23452

ISBN-13: 978-0-9996127-0-5

DEDICATION

This is dedicated to my amazing, loving husband. Without him, I would have never gotten this far. His unconditional support and love has given me wings. His love has given me confidence within myself, encouraging me to be brave enough to write and watch my lifelong dream take off.

I love you, Bryan, always and forever.

JORDIE IN CHARGE

CONTENTS

CHAPTER ONE

Year of Corwaithe—Spring 1223

L ove was something her mother said came once in a lifetime. That love could be felt like a slap to the face because it was that strong. Her mother said that love conquers all, that love can stop wars, and that love is a forever promise between two people.

Jordie could honestly say, out loud to the whole of Castre, that she loved Lane. He was her heart and soul. The joy he brought her was unexplainable in mere words. He was all hers. For the love they shared was a forever promise, just like her mother said.

Jordie quickly dressed, donning a dark green gown that accentuated her figure. She sat on a bench at the end of her bed, pulling on her traveling boots. She called them that even though the only traveling she had ever done was sneaking around outside.

With a smirk, Jordie locked her chamber door. She unlatched the window and pushed it open, peering into the semi-darkness for Lane.

It was not yet dawn. The pinkening of the sky was just spreading across Castre, so there was still time for her to spend with Lane before he had to go report at the end of his watch. The other guards took their turns on the ramparts, but if she slipped out now, no one would see her. Her parents would never know.

Jordie sat on the edge of the windowsill, waiting for Lane to appear. She watched the sun rise in the sky. The pink faded to a brilliant orange, and then to a turquoise blue.

Still he did not appear.

A knock came at her door.

Jordie nearly jumped out of her skin. With a quick turn, she dropped back inside her chamber, closing the window and kicking off her boots.

"Just a minute," she called.

Jordie shoved the boots under her bed. Shifting her long, red hair off to the side, she opened the door.

"Good morning, Father," she said with a smile. "You're awake early this morning."

Her father scowled. "I could say the same to you, Jordie."

Jordie smiled, sleepily giving her eyes a rub. Her father, Robert, peered over her shoulder, looking into her chamber. With a raised eyebrow, he studied her. Jordie covered over a yawn, as if she couldn't hold it back.

Robert's eyes hardened. "I will see you later," he said.

"All right, Da," she replied, getting ready to shut the door.

Robert's left boot caught the edge of the door. "Where are you heading off to?"

Jordie's breath caught in her throat. "I was planning on going for a walk later."

"Where are you going right now?"

"Nowhere," she told him with a shrug, "I am simply trying on dresses to see which ones I still like." She twirled. "What do you think of this one?"

"Fine, if you like green," he said, waving goodbye as he walked away.

Jordie shut the door, letting out the breath she was holding. She locked the door again, heading back over to her bed. Quietly, she got down on her hands and knees, retrieving the boots she had tossed. Then, before she forgot, she slipped the key to her room in her pocket.

Once again, Jordie pulled on her boots, keeping her eye on the door. She tiptoed over to the window and pulled it open, praying that the hinges would not squeak and reveal to the whole of Castre what she was about to do.

Lane was still not down there waiting for her. By the stars! Where was he? His shift must be over by now, so there was no excuse for him being late. That guardsman of hers was going to get it!

Jordie swung her legs over the edge of the window, looking below. It wasn't that far of a fall—at least, not in her eyes. Her younger sister, the prissy Lady Kathleen, might be terrified of heights, but not Jordie.

Below her was a young, slender willow tree. While it was neither tall nor strong, the tree had caught her fall time and time again. Small boulders surrounded the tree. Her mother, Cynthia, lacked the skill of a gardener, so each plant she planted found itself in a ring of stone.

Jordie chuckled. "By Corwaithe, I love you, Mother," she whispered as she looked in amusement at all the plants surrounded in stone.

Jordie waited until she could wait no more. What happened to that man of hers? Was he hurt? Had he finally spoken with her father about them? Or was he detained by someone else? By Corwaithe, that "someone" had better not be a she!

And with that thought, Jordie jumped.

She shoved herself off the ledge, falling with her palms open to catch the branches.

"Shit!" she yelled, closing her eyes as she hit a branch, scratching her face.

With sheer luck, she grabbed hold of one branch, slowing her fall. Then she stopped. Jordie opened her eyes. She was hanging mainly by the fabric of her dress, splayed out over the branches. Her feet were spread wide, as her arms were above her head, holding onto the branch she happened to grab.

Squirming, she made her way down the tree. The climb wasn't as bad as she anticipated it would be. Once on the ground, Jordie began pulling leaves out of her hair, and out of her long, thick dress.

"Blast you, tree," she cursed.

"Of course, blame the tree," a voice said.

Jordie spun in a slow circle, trying to figure out who spoke. "Who goes there?"

"Just an observer of teenage stupidity," the voice said with a laugh.

Jordie rolled her eyes, "No stupidity here, just a woman in love."

Jordie brushed her dress smooth and fixed her hair, braiding it loosely over to the left side. She stood under the willow, patiently waiting in the fresh air for her man. She wasn't worried about whomever the voice belonged to. In fact, she didn't care. No one would keep her from Lane. And nothing was going to scare her away.

Jordie shifted from foot to foot. Her stomach rumbled with hunger. Still Lane wasn't coming. Where was that man? Jordie walked around the castle garden as she waited. If Lane wasn't coming now, then he would definitely be at their usual waiting spot in a little while.

Jordie walked over to a nearby bench and sat down. A giant gray dog lumbered over to her. Jordie began petting the beastie of a dog behind the ears. Jordie looked off to her left, watching to see who passed by the slotted iron gate. She stopped petting the animal, focused on trying to catch a glimpse of her love.

"You are just so interesting," the same deep voice said to her.

Startled, Jordie jumped from the bench.

"Who are you?" she asked.

"Aramoren," he replied.

Jordie blinked.

And there he was—seated on the bench. Aramoren was tall, covered in gray fur, and staring at her with bright, shimmering yellow eyes. Two sharp teeth came down over his bottom lip. Aramoren smiled at her. Jordie didn't want to seem impolite so she smiled back. He seemed like a friendly creature, even if he'd scared the peas out of her pods.

"I've never met a shifter before," Jordie said.

"How would you know if you had?

Jordie put her hands on her hips. "Well, aren't you fun?" she said, rolling her eyes.

Aramoren sighed, rising from the bench. "Oh, the folly of youth," he quipped. "Change is coming your way," he said, circling her.

"So, you say."

"That was very stupid," he said. "You being pregnant and all."

Jordie raised an eyebrow the nosy shifting beast.

"Yes, yes—I hear you. Change is coming," Jordie said. "Lane and I are going to have a baby. He loves me. And we're getting married!"

"Funny, I wouldn't have guessed that at all."

There was something in his tone that she didn't care for. Jordie looked past the shifter, to the iron gate. Lane was not there. Tired of waiting, she trudged off to their usual meeting place, and Aramoren followed.

She looked skyward, seeing if it was yet time. The nooning bell would be tolling soon. Then shortly after that, she would meet Lane. Jordie was going to demand an answer from the man. Never before had Lane kept her waiting like this.

"I hope he is all right," Jordie said.

Aramoren said nothing.

"I love him so much," she told the shifter.

Aramoren sighed again.

"Is that *all* you plan on doing?" Jordie asked, irritated.

"I can tell you love the man. It seeps out of you like pus from an infected wound."

"Oh, how lovely."

"Well, he is waiting! Sally forth, young, incompetent lover!"

"I am not incompetent," Jordie growled back.

Aramoren smiled. "Because falling from your chamber window onto a tree is so intelligent. You don't want to squash your child," Aramoren said, then disappeared before her eyes.

Jordie scowled at the last place she saw the shifter. With a grumble, she made her way to the iron gate. She wasn't going to let the shifter get the better of her.

Jordie stood at the gate, shaking off the experience with Aramoren, before opening the latch.

With a happy smile, and love filling her heart, she made her way to where she knew her handsome guardsman would be waiting for her.

CHAPTER TWO

With a smile on her lips, she snuck under the portcullis to the left side. The watch was always lax there as the castle butted up against the Forgotten Woods. She had done this every day for the past year, right after the nooning meal. Finally free, Jordie skipped merrily to the edge of the forest.

She saw her man waiting for her down by the path entrance into the Forgotten Woods. She never knew why the forest was called so—or if she had, she couldn't remember. But she believed that it was due to all the thick overgrown vegetation that clambered up the trees. The "Forgotten Woods"—such a foreboding name! People like to create drama where there was none, Jordie noted, even if it was simply over a plant-filled forest.

He stood tall and proud in his red tunic, a rose in a patch of dandelions. His strong jaw was set, and a small smile twitched at his lips. Lane Flashew was a sensitive and private man, wanting to keep their love a secret until he saw an opportunity to ask her father—which she hoped would be this morning.

Jordie thought keeping their relationship a secret was a wise idea as her father had grown easily provoked as of late. Plus, she didn't want the whole world knowing just yet.

Being the daughter of a king made affairs of the heart a little more complicated.

Her sweet Lane studied the ground as she approached. Her heart filled with love for this powerful, wonderful man. His arms rippled underneath his tunic. He had seemed to fill out more since she saw him last, which was ridiculous, because that was only yesterday.

The broad smile across her face could not be removed. The love she felt for this man poured out of her heart like a spring. And Lane returned the same love in kind. He often mentioned how he couldn't wait to spend time with her—to make love in the forest or sneak into her chamber. He brought her flowers when he could and always doted on her.

She greeted her man with a kiss on the cheek. "How are you this day?"

"My beautiful, Jordie," he said kissing her forehead, "are you ready to see it all completed today? And I am doing wonderful."

He backed away from her, patting the top of her hand.

She loved everything about this man. From the proud, confident strides of his feet, to the swirling storms of his gray eyes, to the faint freckles on his nose. She loved his thoughtfulness, his attentiveness. She adored everything about the man, and hopefully soon, they would be husband and wife.

Lane dropped her hand and described the home he built for her in the Forgotten Woods. But his attentions to her seemed distracted as he looked away more often than not.

Even though the Castle of Veiled Hills backed up against the enormous forest, her father did not protect it. The forest was a place he deemed out of his jurisdiction because of the vast expanse it covered. He cared not to deal with the peoples or creatures living inside it. He would not risk the lives of his warriors patrolling a forest that could easily hide rabble. Jordie understood his caution.

"Come, Jordie," Lane said, extending his hand. "I want to show you our palace."

They walked together down the forest path, her hand in his thick, calloused one. His size dominated her slender one. He walked with a heavy booted stride, trampling his way down the path like a war horse.

How lucky it was, she thought, that at seventeen she had found the love of her life! She gave Lane's hand a loving squeeze. Love like theirs was a once in a lifetime experience, as her mother said. A true experience that only a few got to call their own, and she was lucky enough to call this man hers. And soon he would be hers forevermore, as he promised.

Lane casually dropped her hand, as he pointed something out to her. But Jordie only had eyes for Lane.

As one of her father's castle guardsmen, Lane Flashew stood watch on the wall from midnight to mid-morning. From her bedroom window, she could admire his noble form during his patrol. Often, she would fall asleep gazing adoringly at him, then wake to find him still there, watching over her, protecting her.

Lane was her everything

On they went, until they came to a small clearing in the middle of the Forgotten Woods. Tall fir trees guarded the small fruit trees, and a footpath led to a creek. Lane pointed it all out as made especially for her. Their home was special, all to themselves, as no one else knew about it. Here they would share their home and raise a family together.

This place was their slice of heaven.

"I love you so much, Dee, and I cannot wait to see our little babe soon," he whispered to her as he walked in front of her through the fruit trees.

"I love you too, Lane," she replied, the sun warming her cream-colored skin. "What should we name our babe?"

"Charlotte, if she is a girl," he said guiding her a little firmly past some low shrubs, "and Liam, if it is a boy." His face drew in seriously, and a shadow passed over his gray eyes. "What do you think?"

"I really like those names," she said, smiling up at him.

"Today, I petitioned your father for your hand."

"Really?" she asked, clinging to his neck and raining kisses on him. "Oh, Lane, I am so excited!"

Lane stood still for a few moments, gazing at her with a fixed, blank expression before pulling the last large branch out of her way, revealing to her their home.

Jordie's mouth dropped open in awe as she viewed their home for the first time. The roof was wooden, not thatched with hay like the ones from the village. The windows were trimmed in wood to help keep in the heat. Flowering buds blooming on the nearby fruit trees.

A small breeze went by, rustling through her braided hair and shifting the hems of her dress. Not a single detail escaped Jordie's eye. Her potted plants waited outside the doors. Boxes for flowers decorated the windows. The oaken door even had a willow tree carved into it with a dark ornate iron handle.

She couldn't believe that Lane made this amazing window-paned cottage with his own two hands. How unbelievable that a guardsman could get all of this done! He had started building their home when she told him she was with child. He told her he wanted a place of their own, away from the busyness of the castle, to raise their babe in quiet, blissful solitude. But that was four months ago, and this is what he had done by himself.

Jordie knelt down by the cottage door, smelling her little flowers. She had potted those in her room and had only brought them outside yesterday to get more sun, leaving them on the landing outside the double doors into the dining hall. Their little petals were a dazzling golden yellow and bright red. Jordie knelt on the ground to smell them, knowing that far too soon, she would be too big to bend.

With a smile, she opened the door to their new home. It was a fine, sturdy home. It was a small cottage, no bigger than her chamber, but then again, her room at home was large and grander than what most had.

Jordie peeked inside, admiring the polished hardwood floors. There was a small kitchen about six feet long with a sink. Cabinets lined the kitchen above the sink, giving her plenty of storage for things. A dining table and chairs stood to her right. The small round table had a cloth on top of it, which she thought was rather thoughtful of Lane.

A big fireplace was behind her, on the left-hand side of the cottage wall. The bedroom they would share was behind the fire-place. A loft was to the right, with a ladder built into the wall.

Jordie smiled as she looked at it all. It was so perfect. It was so grand. The smile that creased her lips broadened as she appreciated everything he had accomplished.

Jordie almost yelped as she saw a giant gray dog laying on the other side of the kitchen table by the wall. She walked over and petted the shaggy beast, giving it praises, before heading outside. The animal looked just like the one she'd seen a few hours before—but she let that thought slide for now, she was just so happy.

With an excited breath, she stepped outside to walk around. Lane had built a one-horse stall and a lean-to for wood. There was already a lot of wood under the lean-to as well, which would be nice for the coming winter.

She loved it out here. Away from the hustle and bustle of the castle life. In fact, she couldn't see a hint of the castle from where she was. What a relief to get away from her sister Maggie's wedding preparations, and the chaos of five younger sisters. Out here, she had peace. It was made even better with Lane, her one and only, who would be by her side through it all.

Jordie couldn't wait for her father to give his blessing. She was sure he would. Lane was a good, loyal man with a great work ethic. He was an excellent marksman and wielded his sword with finesse. Living out here, he was more than capable of protecting her and their baby.

Jordie sat on the front door step with a contented sigh, admiring the forest and her little flowers. She was so grateful to her husband-to-be. He had accomplished so much in such a short amount of time. She sat there for a while, the sun shining in her face.

"Like it?" Lane asked.

"I love it."

Lane helped her off the ground and she dusted herself. Happily, she turned the iron knob and opened the cottage door again. Jordie immediately noticed that the large gray dog was gone. She had not noticed before, but most of her things had already been brought inside. They were stacked neatly on the cushioned chair that was in front of the fireplace. She remembered packing a small bag of clothes last night to give to Lane, but did not remember taking her favorite blanket or pillow. She left those in her room this morning.

In fact, she didn't remember doing any of this.

He did say he'd already asked her mother and father for her hand. Had they said yes? Or perhaps he just assumed that her father would agree, and so he'd brought everything down ahead of time. Lane knew she was sick most mornings, and being as sick as she was, she found she had trouble remembering some things.

Lane asked. He'd said so.

Inside, butterflies of excitement tickled her belly.

Lane stood in the doorway. "I brought those things down this morning," he explained with his arms crossed.

"That was very sweet of you!"

"I even bought supplies. They are put away in the cupboards."

Jordie walked over to the kitchen, still in wonder at it all. It was the first time she had seen the completed project. Every other time she asked about their home, he had given vague answers. But clearly, the suspense was worth the wait. Pure joy delighted her silly. She never imagined being so happy. All of this was for them, and the baby.

And kind Lane, her sweet and thoughtful husband-to-be, took care of her so well. She didn't think anything of him bringing her things down for her so she wouldn't have to. He stocked their small house so she wouldn't have to go to the village if she got too sick with the babe. Lane was the kindest man she knew.

She walked from the kitchen to the two chairs that sat by the fireplace. The hearth was empty, but the early spring morning was too warm for one, anyway. To the right of the fireplace was a ladder going up to the loft, and to the left of that was the bedroom door.

Jordie peeked behind the bedroom door. There was a small room with a bed just barely big enough for them both. A small chest waited at the foot of the bed for her clothes, but there wasn't one for Lane. Evidently, he'd only been thinking of her.

"Oh Lane, it is so wonderful!"

"I am glad you think so."

His tone surprised her. All day long, he'd seemed hurried, which was not like him at all. And now as he stood before her, he looked agitated. His arms were crossed and his brow furrowed. He kicked the wooden floor, scuffing his boot.

"Everything all right, darling?" she ventured.

"Aye," he replied, scratching the back of his head. His face relaxed a bit. "I am going to go ask your father for a response now."

With that, he turned heel and left. His sudden change of demeanor worried her. Was something not going according to his plan? Had something gone wrong?

Likely he was just concerned about asking her father for her hand. After all, King Robert Duvoir was a particular man—an endearing man, but particular. Robert liked things done a certain way, his way, and he also liked to make his wealth and position known. And Lane did say that was where he was going.

Jordie resolved to stay in the cottage for a while longer before making her way back up to the castle. Just to give the men time to talk, and time for her father to say yes.

It was already the best day!

JORDIE IN CHARGE

CHAPTER THREE

J ordie waited until most of the afternoon was gone. The sun was starting to slip behind the castle as she made her way back to Veiled Hills. The leaves appeared golden on the breeze, and fading light flickered through the branches.

Jordie walked up the small sloping hill towards the castle. The green grass and the sprinkling of spring flowers poked their way up out of the once frozen ground. It was a wondrous time of year, her favorite in fact, as the trees blossomed with pink blooms and the hatchlings crept out of their shells.

Finally, she stood under the portcullis. The gray stone shimmered under the fading light. Each handcrafted rectangle of stone was expertly placed, creating something magnificent. Under the gate sat a gray dog, staring back at her. Jordie smiled at the beast before walking towards her home.

Home.

One simple word brought a smile to her face as she trudged merrily into the keep.

Jordie went past the thick double doors and through the long, wide dining hall and up the curved staircase. The royal bedchambers lined the right side of the hallway with her parents' room on the very end. The left side bedchambers were for guests.

Everything was eerily silent as Jordie walked past Maggie's door which was, as usual, open. And also, as usual, Maggie sat at her easel painting away, like nothing in Castre was amiss. But no laughter from Myah or Jenny could be heard from the hallway. Robert was not bellowing at someone, which was odd. More often than not, he was growling about something not getting done.

Korah wasn't teasing Kathleen about the obsessive perfectionism she shared with their mother. Melanie wasn't there to pick sides. Everything inside the castle was as silent as a graveyard.

The hairs on the back of her neck stood on end.

Jordie hugged herself tight as she came closer to her chamber door. Something prickled at the back of her neck. It didn't feel right. She thought mayhap it was because she was pregnant, but this was a different feeling. She didn't feel the sudden urge to dash for a bucket. Something was off.

Now that she thought about it, Lane never came back to tell her the good news that Father approved of the marriage. In fact, he hadn't been acting right all morning. He seemed hurried and tense. Angry, almost.

Jordie cautiously approached her chamber. And now she knew why something felt so irregular. The door was wide open. Hadn't she left it locked? She walked into the middle of her room to find it devoid of any furniture. Everything was bare, as bare as could be. Silently, she stood in her room confused. She had only been gone a few hours.

What could change in such a short amount of time?

Footsteps echoed down the hallway. She recognized the heavy footfalls of her father. Then he stood in the doorframe, hands on his hips.

"Care to tell me anything, Jordie?" His tone was serious, laced with mounting fury.

"Wish to tell you what, Da?" she asked politely.

"Do not toy with me, young lady. I know what happened."

"Did Lane not ask you?"

Her father's face fell. He looked as confused as she felt. "Ask me what, Jordie?"

With tears springing in her eyes, she said, "Lane said he asked you for my hand this morning."

King Robert closed his eyes, disappointment clouding his face. "Lane is gone," her father said, coming towards her. "He said you are carrying a child, and that he was leaving. He has been taken care of."

Robert stood over her, his face a mask of stone. Tears prickled Jordie's eyes. Her knees threatened to give out underneath her.

"What do you mean, taken care of?" she asked.

"He is gone," her father replied flatly. "Trusted men took him far away from us, and you."

"He said he was going to marry me! He even built us a cottage," she said with a pleading look at her father.

"Corwaithe, Jordie!" He shook his head in sheer anger. "You are such a disgrace."

"I loved him, Da," Jordie cried, "and he left me!"

Robert grabbed her by the arm. "Damn it all, Jordie, look at what you have done!"

"I loved him," she wailed. "What am I to do?"

"Get out! Go live in that cottage he built you and do not come back, you utter embarrassment! You're dead to us now, and no one needs to know of your disgrace."

"But, Da," Jordie cried.

Robert slapped her across the face. "You," he yelled, "have no right to call me *your* father!"

Jordie touched her bleeding lip.

"You are nothing but a whore, Jordie! I raised you better than that, and this is the thanks I receive for giving you life, clothes on your back, and everything you have ever wanted or desired? You go out and get yourself with child with the first man to come along? You are lucky I am not casting you out of Veiled Hills completely, or better yet, making *you* disappear. So, go! And don't come back!"

"Da . . ."

Robert grabbed her again and threw her out the door. Jordie landed on her side, careful of her small rounding belly. She scrambled to her feet, standing as far away from her father as possible. What now? Fear washed over her as she thought about her life and that of the child she carried.

"You are a disappointment to me, your mother, your sisters, this family, our people, and the family name. You are a slut, a whore, a common bar wench that I had the misfortune of conceiving. Do not come back to this keep unless you are summoned."

Stunned, she looked at her father, bewildered.

And there were her sisters, standing at the doorway with their heads down, not looking at her. Jordie could feel their shame as if they had slapped her themselves. They refused to meet her eye. They refused to speak her name, to console her.

"Mum?" Jordie whispered.

Queen Cynthia turned her back on her daughter, staring down the hallway as sobs shook her slender frame.

Jordie began to panic, her world tipped on end. She called out to every sister by name, pleading them for one of them to intervene on her behalf, but all stayed silent.

Her own mother had her back to her. Jordie fell silent. Her own flesh and blood had abandoned her when she needed them the most. No one looked at her. No one said a word to her as they parted ways for her to pass. Jordie hugged herself tightly as she walked through them and down the staircase.

The castle felt like it was spinning. Her hurt body ached, but she didn't notice it as much as she did the urge to flee. This wasn't what she had pictured. Her stomach began to churn; she felt like she was going to retch. She didn't look anyone in the eye as she kept walking out of the dining hall, leaving this place for good.

Her father bellowed behind her as she neared the doors, "From this moment forward, no one is allowed to talk to that woman. She will be permitted to live in Veiled Hills, but as an outsider to this clan."

Plunging through the double doors, Jordie started to weep. Her life was over. She was an outcast in her own clan, she and her child.

She began to panic.

Jordie ran past the gray dog sitting in the middle of the castle yard.

Faster and faster she ran from the castle, through the grass, down the small knoll, and along the trail leading back to her little home, for it was all she had left. It was all she had left of anything. Sorrow settled in her heart.

How am I going to feed myself? I do not know how to hunt. I have no coin. I have no one. How am I going to be able to provide for us both? I didn't plan on this!

She reached the cottage door and yanked it open, then slammed it behind her. She paced and paced. Her small home didn't leave much room for pacing. Jordie paced so much she swore she was wearing a trail in the lacquered pine floorboards.

After a while, Jordie stopped. Nothing was going to fix this mess that Lane left her in. He lied. He had lied to her this entire time, and she was stupid enough to fall for it. Her face burned with tears and regret. Was any man what he portrayed himself to be? First, Lane and now her own father. They'd both stabbed her in the back.

Oh, my Goddess, how stupid could I be? she thought. *My parents, who told me for years that their love was unconditional, have lied to me. Lane, that son of a bitch, has lied to me. Men are all liars. I will never trust one again! I so swear, I never will.*

She cried a little more but this time out of frustration at her own gullibility.

Jordie dried her eyes and climbed the ladder into the loft, curious as to how big it was. There she found a bassinet and a wooden crate beside it. She thought it peculiar that Lane would make her one. It seemed like such a kind gesture.

She snorted derisively.

Jordie pushed the crate over to the other side of the loft and carefully pulled down the bassinet. It was crafted from Birchwood and polished to a shine. Inside, there were linens, cloths for the babe's bottom, small dressing clothes, a small stuffed toy, and a note.

She set aside the note and opened the crate. Tears welled in her eyes again, but she suppressed them. Inside she found a few of her nicer dresses from when she was younger and two jeweled necklaces. She tucked it all away for later.

Jordie picked up the note.

You will need this. Good luck.

– Mother

Jordie sobbed.

Lane must have told them this morning before they went on their walk. He must have! It made her heart sick. He had planned this all along. He planned to leave her and the baby they made together.

She walked woodenly to her new room, the room he made for just her, lay down on her new bed, and cried into the quilt, until she resolved herself to never let a cheating, lying, horrible person destroy her again. She would be strong for this babe. She vowed to protect him or her, to shield it from the lies of the world.

•••••

She woke up groggily, her eyes adjusting to the dim light. She looked around, forgetting where she was, but when she remembered all that had happened, she sat up and steeled herself. Jordie had to be strong for her baby. There was no other choice.

Jordie walked into the kitchen looking for water to make tea. It took her a few tries to get the fire going, but she managed. Within a couple of minutes, she had tea that wasn't hot but was palatable to drink. It calmed her stomach only slightly.

She stood before the fire, glaring at it. Jordie had once thought herself to be a woman any man would be lucky to have. But she had proven to be a woman that a man found easy to use. Never again would she let someone use her.

26

The fire flickered and whipped in front of her as she gazed into its inviting warmth. She reflected about how she used to be carefree, vibrant, and happy. Now, she was a shell of her former self. Her hurt went so deep. These new wounds and anger at being abandoned were something she knew she would need years to overcome. Her trust in people was broken.

Jordie turned to stare out the window. The castle was just beyond the woods, about a twenty-minute walk. She glared at the window, at the whole structure that Lane had built to keep her inside.

Tomorrow morning, when the sun came up, she would prepare what she needed to store away, for when the babe came into this world. More than likely, it would just be her and her child until she either died here or had enough coin to move away forever. She was in control now, and no one was going to take that away from her.

With hard eyes and a determined heart, she went back into her room to lay down and get a good night's rest. She was going to need it come the morning.

JORDIE IN CHARGE

CHAPTER FOUR

Year of Corwaithe –- Fall 1223

It was five months now since he left her all alone. Five months of being disowned. Five long, lonely months of no one. No one around her to talk to besides the stray dog that had wandered onto her property and never left. So, Jordie took him in. He was the only loyal creature in her life, and to be honest with herself, she liked it that way.

She had learned to like the solitude. It took some getting used to. At first, she thought she was going to go crazy. For the first few weeks, she wanted more than anything to go back to the castle and beg her parents to take her in, to forgive her. Then she admitted to herself that her family wanted it this way, and there was nothing she could say to sway their minds.

Instead, she learned to thrive. To care for herself without the help of anyone around her. And she would continue to be the best she could be for her child. Jordie wove baskets to catch fish and store berries and roots. She did whatever she could do to eat each day.

She was a bullheaded woman. Lane left her a bow and a quiver of arrows. Each day, she practiced a little more. And each day, she pulled the bow back a little farther and got closer and closer to her mark.

Jordie sighed.

She walked through her forest, scanning every tree branch and low brush for easy prey like rabbit, squirrel, or even a broeshilak. It was becoming increasingly more difficult to walk these days. It seemed like she blossomed overnight and waddled like a duck wherever she went.

She had to let out all her dresses. And every one had holes in it. Even the fabric seemed heavier against her sore body. It was hard to get out of her chair by the hearth. It was harder to get out of bed. It was certainly the most difficult to put on her boots, so most of the time she just went to sleep with them on.

It took her a while to figure out how to hunt with a knife. She practiced for hours outside, throwing it against the lean-to from to a distance. It took her even longer to figure out how to skin an animal without cutting into the precious meat. But she was getting better every day. She didn't have much of a choice if she wanted to eat and live.

Jordie clucked her tongue, and the beast of a dog came bounding back to her. She patted Ranger on the head, praising the giant beast, happy that Corwaithe sent her a friend when she truly needed one.

Jordie knelt down and kissed her big dog on the nose, telling him how thankful she was for him being around. Ranger wagged his tail and nuzzled at her legs with his nose.

Twigs snapped in the distance.

She froze, looking towards the sound.

Ranger wagged his tail. Jordie patted him quietly on the head before striding forward, bow drawn. Carefully, she walked towards the sound, peering through the bushes. A doe was eating leaves off a low branch.

She had never killed a deer before. She didn't even know what to do with it once it was down. Usually she only felled squirrels, rabbits, and sometimes the dumb broeshilak. She had killed the occasional groewindel—a giant wild bird with colorful plumage and a shrieking, echoing call. They were said to be magical, but the only magical thing she got from it was a few days' worth of food.

She stared at the doe for a long time, watching it nibble on the leaves, debating whether she wanted to end its life. It was food. It would be a lot of food. The meat would be able to feed her for a long time, especially if she smoked it all. She nocked an arrow.

Carefully she moved the bushes blocking her clean shot.

Ranger lay behind her, waiting patiently. His ears were back in annoyance, but he remained quiet.

Jordie blew out a frustrated breath. This was too much work for her to do. She walked away from the animal and headed back to her small, warm home.

"Another day, my friend," she called to the doe.

Jordie sighed.

More than anything, she wanted meat to sustain her and this child, but she knew her limits, and this deer was going to be a big project that she couldn't handle on her own just yet.

Jordie walked the trampled path back to her cottage, waddling and huffing along. From the trees, birds tweeted their songs of the brilliant late afternoon sun. But beyond the treetops, gray clouds loomed.

Jordie grumbled.

It was already hot, and rain would make it muggy. Her dress clung to her body more as she walked. Jordie walked past the two fallen logs that marked the halfway point home when she caught movement out of the corner of her eye.

A broeshilak, a tiny six-legged creature, the same size as a wiener pig, stood on its hind legs on the closest log to her. It sniffed the air with its rabbit-like nose. Its long ears twitched toward her. Broeshilak meat was delicious and more sustaining than that of a black deer. With careful precision, she nocked an arrow. Ranger whined at her side, but she released it anyway.

It struck the creature right through the neck. It dropped like a stone, rolling dead onto the path. She sent a sign of thanks up to the Goddess Corwaithe for blessing her with this fine meat and a quick kill. She didn't know what she would have done if she had not have gotten it.

All the while, she had a strange feeling, like something wasn't settling right in her gut. It felt heavy. It felt achy. Her thighs hurt and her muscles hurt with an occasional odd spasm as she bent down to pick up the fallen creature.

Jordie brushed it off.

She must be working herself too hard. But she needed food for her and her babe. Jordie walked as briskly as she could, trying to get back before the dark clouds overtook her. An early fall storm was brewing, and when they came, they came fast.

Ranger bounded off ahead.

She didn't realize how far she ventured until she finally caught sight of her home. She breathed out a sigh of relief. Sweat dripped from her brow.

"Oh, Ranger," she said tiredly, as she neared her home, "this creature is so heavy."

Ranger barked, pulling her by the hems of her dress towards the door.

"All right, boy, let's get this nice dinner ready," she called to him as she entered the house, setting the animal down on the counter.

Ranger continued to bark at her. She couldn't understand why. He kept pulling on her, trying to get her to go into her bedroom, but she couldn't. She had an animal to skin and take care of. She couldn't let it spoil.

Ranger began growling at her, but she chastised him for being a brat. He whined and pawed at her. He barked, snapped, and bared his teeth. Still she ignored him, continuing to skin the broeshilak on the kitchen counter, and yelling at him to calm his shit.

Jordie opened the animal on its underbelly. She took out the innards and set them aside for Ranger. She worked

33

quickly as the pains in her belly worsened. Jordie was having a hard time remaining standing. Soon the animal was completely skinned. Her next step was to slice the meat and salt it.

Jordie wiped off her hands and got the drying racks down from the loft. Ranger barked angrily at her for going up there, but no one else was here to get it, and she told him so.

Her dog only grumbled.

Jordie tied the meat to the racks just as the thunder roared, bellowing its anger. Lightening flashing across Corwaithe's heavens. A roaring boom—she jumped. The thunder was closer than she realized.

With an arduous waddle, she walked out to the horse stall. Jordie dug a small hole in the ground for the fire. With tired hands, she stacked the kindling and hit the flint to her knife. Soon the wood was blazing. Jordie added green wood to it, causing the fire to smoke. Doggedly, she got up off the ground, dusting herself off. She brought the meat rack outside and placed it over the smoking fire.

Jordie was absolutely exhausted.

Her feet were so swollen. She could feel the pinch inside her boots, and she was desperately thirsty, but she couldn't stop until this was done. It would be her food when the babe came. It would be all she would have for a while. She couldn't stop working.

At least not yet.

She felt the long pain in her belly worsen, continuing for a few moments and then stopping, but it wasn't enough to keep her from moving. Jordie refused to quit.

Again, and again the pains came, but she knew she couldn't stop. The meat couldn't be allowed to spoil. Jordie hung the meat over the fire and put more green leaves and wood on the fire.

Only after the last rack of meat swayed over the smoking flames of her fire did she go inside to rest. She got a fire going in her own small hearth then collapsed in the cushioned chair. She was too tired to get something for Ranger to eat. She was too tired to do anything for herself.

Ranger whimpered as he nudged her hand with his cold black nose. He put his mouth over her boots, trying to pull them off for her. Jordie untied them as Ranger continued pulling with great effort.

"I am sorry, boy," she cooed to the hairy gray beast. "I am just so tired."

He licked her hand and laid his shaggy head at her feet.

With the heat of the flames, Jordie was soon asleep in the chair.

JORDIE IN CHARGE

CHAPTER FIVE

I t wasn't long before she woke. The pain in her pregnant belly was unbearable. Between the thundering rain and her exhaustion, she was absolutely miserable.

And she wet the chair.

"Oh shit," she said, stumbling up.

Ranger wouldn't stop whining at her, licking her legs and feet, pulling at her to go towards her bedroom. She wanted to send him for help, but she was an outcast. No one would come. And the clans-people wouldn't know whose dog he was. No one would know where to find her.

She was utterly alone in this.

Jordie got out of the soaking wet chair, grabbed onto the support beam in the middle of cottage, and unknowingly pushed.

Then it suddenly dawned on her that her babe was coming.

Jordie remembered her mother giving birth to her youngest sister, Melanie. She remembered her mother clutching the wooded frame at the end of the bed, dripping in sweat with her legs spread wide, as she explained what was going to be happening. Her mother pushed as she gripped the end of the bed, a woman's hands underneath her to catch her baby sister. Maggie watched in shock, turning green, but Jordie watched with fascination as her youngest sister came into the world.

"Oh shit," she repeated again as another contraction overcame her.

She assumed she had overexerted herself, because she truly did. Taking down that animal, then working relentlessly to cure the meat, did a number on her body. Now it all was catching up to her, and the babe was coming soon. Jordie looked helplessly around, not knowing what to get or where to go.

"Ranger," she called panting, clinging to the beam in the middle of the cottage, fingernails digging into the wood, "get my blanket, boy. Please."

The ever-faithful beast ran into her room and drug back the quilted blanket that her mother, Maggie, and herself made once upon a time. Jordie put the blanket underneath her quaking body.

As the thunder rumbled, Jordie squatted down on her knees and pushed. She spread her legs wide, allowing the babe to come, but hanging low enough to not hurt it. She pushed and pushed for what felt like hours.

Sweat fell into her eyes; her body shook with drained, over-worked muscles. She leaned her tired head against the beam and cried. In the darkness of her home, all alone on a storming night, she would give birth to this child and raise it all by herself.

Jordie changed her position slowly, moving so that her back was leaning against the beam, with her legs spread wide.

How will I know what to do? she asked herself. *Goddess guide me.*

"Push," a male voice said to her.

Jordie looked around for the voice but found no one.

"Push."

"Who is there?" she asked, scared.

"Does it really matter?" he scoffed. "I warned you before of change."

As another pain overcame her, Jordie cried, clutching the beam behind her head, and pushed. It was a long one this time. She pushed as hard and as long as she could. Then she felt something slip out from inside of her.

"Easy now," he said.

Jordie slumped against the beam, disoriented, looking at a man with Ranger's ears staring at her. He held her babe in his arms, wiping the birth from its face. She blinked a few times. Was she seeing this right?

Dazed, she stared at the man-dog. He had enormous golden eyes, staring back at her, and large pointed teeth that came out and over his bottom lip. His coloring was dark gray, unlike anything she had ever seen. But she was too exhausted to keep her eyes open.

"I am going to press on your belly to get out the after-birth," the dog-man said.

He held the babe in one arm as he pushed on her belly with the other. She felt the sack and cord inside of her gush out. Ranger placed her babe on her chest. Jordie stared at her perfect, little baby as the man's footfalls echoed around her.

"Thank you, Ranger," she said, hazily.

"My name is Aramoren," he said, coming back to her after disposing of her baby's sack, "and you have been living in my house."

"I'm sorry," she apologized, becoming slightly less conscious, "I didn't know."

"I am aware. No matter," he said, placing a blanket over her from out of nowhere. "I will get my house back soon enough."

Jordie felt his hands right her body against the beam. She was exhausted from everything that happened today, from picking the last of the berries off the vines, to hiking for food, and finally giving birth. Her body had had enough.

She felt something zap her body with shining blue-white fire. Aramoren caressed the child on the head as she held him in her arms. She took the corner of her blanket, wiping the small face to clear his little nose and mouth.

She wriggled herself upright against the beam. Whatever Aramoren had done, she felt more alert and was thankful that he was here.

"He is handsome," Aramoren remarked. "But more importantly, he will grow up to be wise."

Jordie cried.

Her son was here because of help from this man.

Jordie looked up to thank the man for helping her, but all she found was her dog staring back at her. Jordie blinked rapidly, wondering where in Castre a man could disappear to. She called his name, but not a sound came back at her, only a baby's cries and a dog's panting.

Ranger lay at her feet, looking with loving yellow eyes at her son.

She cleaned her baby boy off with her blanket the best she could. Jordie refolded the blanket, laying him down on the clean side. Leaning forward, she untied the back of her dress, pulling herself out of it to expose her breasts. She was thankful to her mother for showing her this with her baby sister, Melanie.

Jordie brought the babe to her breast. Greedily, he began to suckle, closing his small, perfect eyes. She grabbed his tiny left hand, counting the fingers, feeling his softness. He was perfect. He was all hers, made from her, given as a gift from Corwaithe. He was the greatest gift of her life.

It was at this pinnacle moment that she realized why this had happened to her. She was meant to be his mother, to love and protect him unconditionally. Truly unconditionally, not for the sometimes, but for all the time, mistakes or no. Her son was a baby, born of circumstance, born from her, made of her, and born to be loved.

She never knew what she was made of until her father cast her out. She never knew she could hunt, fish, skin an animal, and provide not only for herself but for her babe too. Without those everyday tasks of chopping wood, hunting,

41

and gathering, she wouldn't have grown so strong. From this moment forward, she knew she could survive without a man.

She had just birthed a baby!

And all of this all happened for a reason.

Now the babe depended on her, and she would never let him down. He was her greatest pride and joy. And forevermore, he would always be. Her babe would always come first. She would raise this boy into a fine young man. She would teach him to help others, to help women in need, to not judge anyone for their past but to help them succeed for a better future. She would raise this boy into a man who was truthful, loyal, and who respected women. A man that all other men would strive to be like.

Lane wanted to name you Liam, she recalled.

Jordie snorted.

She was going to name him whatever she wanted because she was on her own, and the boy was hers, not his. A true man wouldn't have left. A true man would have stuck around to help her raise this child. A true man wouldn't have done what Lane Flashew did. But there were no true men around. There were no true men, period.

It was just her.

She would have to do her best for her son now.

Jordie looked down at the beautiful sleeping boy. "What to name you, my sweetling?" she cooed to the babe. "I am going to name you Boden, my little one." She smiled at him. "Aye, my little Boden."

Jordie carefully got up, her clothes around her waist. She made her way slowly to her bedroom. She was tired, but she also needed to clean herself off. She laid the sleeping Boden on the bed, putting a cloth around his little bottom, and dressed him in a small tunic her mother had left for her. Once he was dressed, she swaddled him in a blanket and placed him in the bassinet she brought down from the loft all those months ago. Jordie moved him close to the fire to keep warm while she went outside to get water.

It was raining now, coming down in fierce sheets. Thankfully, it wasn't as cold as she thought it would be. She stripped off her clothes and began washing herself in the rain, using her shift as a washcloth. She washed away the blood and sweat along with everything else that clung to her.

Back at the cottage, Ranger sat in the doorway, guarding them all. If Ranger were a man, he could protect them, but unfortunately for her, he wasn't. She believed she hallucinated that he was, but he was only a dog. There would never be a man in their lives.

Not now, not ever.

She walked naked over to where the meat was smoking. She added more green wood so the fire would go until morning. She was thankful the meat wouldn't spoil. Stiffly, she walked back into her house. Boden still slept next to the crackling fire.

Still naked, Jordie grabbed the blanket off the back of a chair and laid it on the floor beside the fire and her baby. She curled up, her arm tucked under her head, and allowed her body to finally rest.

JORDIE IN CHARGE

CHAPTER SIX

Year of Corwaithe –- Seven Years Later, Winter 1230

Boden had his seventh birthday on the last day of summer, just as the last of the vegetables were harvested and the fall crops ripened before winter struck with its frosty grip. He had grown so tall over the summer and was now stocky like his grandfather.

She couldn't believe that seven years had come and gone so fast. It was now nearly winter at that. Jordie was twenty-five years old. She celebrated her winter birthday alone, without any friend save her son and faithful dog. Good old Ranger looked like he hadn't aged a day.

Her parents never inquired about their grandson. However, they were nice enough to let him come to the village school house to learn his numbers and letters. Her father wanted every child in Veiled Hills to at least know the basics. That was one good thing he did for everyone, and Boden so enjoyed going to learn. His teacher would send him home with a book, and he would go back a few days later with it finished. It warmed her heart to see him pouring over his books.

Boden was also big enough to sleep in the loft. He even acquired, through means of mucking out stalls for the Clemmen family, two playful kittens. Her son was a hardy boy, built thick and tall. He didn't resemble Lane much, save for the gray eyes. Boden was built more like her father, tall like a fir tree but thicker than a castle wall.

The only thing she regretted was not being able to provide more for her son. Aye, she cooked, cleaned, hunted, gathered, was a healer, a teacher, and much more. But she couldn't give him coins for sweets, or a toy or anything else his simple heart desired. She was able to sell her smoked meat occasionally, but the coins went to necessities, and Boden was always left wondering what a taffy would taste like, or a sugared bun.

It broke her heart to tell him no so often.

Jordie walked to the small window to peek outside at her son. Their cow was still in the stall to the left of the window. When she looked to her right, she saw that he was busy playing with Ranger, and this small little something bounding up and down in between.

Curious, she went outside.

"Bo, what is that?"

Boden smiled happily. "It's a puppy, Mum. Harrison Fisher gave him to me since Ranger is getting on in years."

Ranger snorted, his ears flat against his head.

Jordie crossed her arms. "Are you telling me the truth, or shall I go ask?"

"It's the truth, Mum," he told her earnestly. "He gave the pup to me and said it is because I don't have a da."

Jordie closed her eyes in shame but only for a moment. Anger overcame her.

How dare that man tell my son what he does, and doesn't have! she thought.

She closed the door behind her, ready to walk into that village to have a talk with that man.

Jordie fastened the belt on her trews tighter, double-checked the knife and ax in her belt, then whistled for Ranger. The old dog obediently got up to come alongside her.

She glanced over at her son, who now had the small pup in his arms and a curious look on his face.

"Go inside, Boden. I will be back soon," she told him.

Boden nodded. "Mum," he called out, "how come I don't have a father, and everyone else does?"

Jordie stopped dead in her tracks.

All the flame and fury was knocked right out of her. She turned around to look at her small son with his furrowed brows and mop of dark hair.

Jordie sighed. *It is time he knew what happened.*

Her son was smart enough to comprehend. He was old enough to know the reason, but would he hate her? Would he turn away from her as well? Would he understand what happened—what it all meant for them both?

Jordie sighed again, tucking her dark red hair behind her ear.

Her will to fight Harrison Fisher dissolved. Harrison wasn't a mean man, or intentionally cruel. He was a kind man who often spoke honestly, if sometimes out of turn. Right now, making time for Boden was more important. Right now, she needed to tell her son everything and somehow hope that he still loved her.

"Boden," she said, "leave the pup with Ranger, and let's talk inside, sweetling."

Boden set the pup down and opened the cottage door. He took a seat at the kitchen table. He waited for her to shut the door and take a chair opposite of him. He was an obedient child which made talks like this a little better. But still, her heart pounded and sweat covered her palms.

She hadn't talked about Lane in years. She hadn't talked about her parents, her family, or what happened to her with anyone. Aye, she would talk to a dog, but a dog doesn't speak back. A dog listened without judgement, and Ranger was an excellent listener, even if he did sometimes walk away mid-sentence.

Here goes nothing, she thought.

She took his hand in hers. "I was seventeen years old at the time and madly in love with a man, your father. His name is Lane Flashew. He was a guardsman at your grandfather's castle." She paused to let that sink in.

"So," he looked at her puzzled a little. "So, I have a grandpa and a grandma?"

"Yes, sweets, my parents, King Robert and Queen Cynthia Duvoir."

His eyes grew wider. "And they are the king and queen?"

"Yes," she said firmly.

Boden nodded, his eyes wide and curious. "Then what happened?"

"Well, your father, Lane, told me that since I was pregnant with you, he was going to marry me, and we would live happily ever-more as a family here in this cottage." There was a sting in her eyes, but she blinked it away. "He said he asked my father to marry me, but instead, he told my parents a lie. Then he left Veiled Hills."

Boden looked down at his lap. "Does that mean he left because of me?"

Jordie let some tears fall but pulled herself together. "Nay, love, he left because he wasn't man enough to be a father. Any man can get a woman pregnant and call himself a man, but a true man, a real man, stays and becomes a father. And it also goes for others like women who accept and love another man's children. Mayhap someday, when I meet the right man and fall in love, he will take you as a son and be your father. That is also a true man."

"So, a man is someone who does right when others turn away?" he asked her with his enormous, cloudy gray eyes.

"Aye, and a man is someone who steps up when others step away."

Boden was silent for a moment. She held his hand with her one hand, and wrapped the other around him, stroking his head. He was her everything. She would do anything for him.

It was unfair for him to be without a father, but she couldn't help it. She loved Lane once upon a time. She thought they would live happily ever after, but things didn't work out that way. And sadly, her son, her sweet Boden, had to live with the consequences of his father's weaknesses.

After a while Boden looked up at her and asked, "Then what happened?"

"Well, your grandpa wasn't happy," Jordie said. "He said a few very mean things to me and told me not to come back."

"Is that it?"

"Aye, love, that is the story."

"So," he paused, "what about my father, Lane?"

She smiled wanly at her son. "I never heard from him or saw him again."

"Will I see him again?"

"I hope not, sweetling. He doesn't deserve to get to know you. But someday, you will have a father who loves you. This I do so promise," Jordie said with a hug.

Boden beamed at her. "You mean it?"

"Aye, I mean it," she smiled.

"Will he take me fishing?"

She laughed softly. "Well, I already take you fishing."

"Aye, and you're a good one, Mum, but can my new da take me fishing?"

Jordie kissed him on the head. "Yes, sweets, but not if you're constantly covered in dirt."

Boden looked at his hands and arms. "I am a bit dirty."

"Go wash, babe. Dinner will be ready soon."

She kissed him on the clean cheek and sent him out the door. Again, the cottage door slammed for the eighteenth time that day, after she told him not to seventeen times before. She let out a sigh of relief.

He'd taken all the information better than she thought possible. And it saddened her that he wanted something, again—this time something as simple as a father—that she couldn't give him. It's not like she didn't want to have a man in her life.

The men here knew about her. They would speak to her, kindly sometimes. But she could tell that they had made up their minds about her, judged her in one way or another, just as she did them.

She thought it hurtful. The Goddess said that if one man judged another, he should be judged in equal measure. But no one seemed to heed that little piece of advice from the highest power in the land, the Goddess who governed over all peoples. Even Jordie struggled to remember it. Although when Corwaithe first came to Castre and decreed that everyone was of equal measure, people would cling to Corwaithe's statement. But that wisdom dimmed over the years.

To her, Corwaithe's meaning of "equal measure" meant that love was love, no matter the social difference between two people. But four hundred years had passed, and forgetfulness had polluted Corwaithe's world. No one believed that love came in equal measure anymore.

Her father was living proof that love was never merely love but an arrangement of finances. And many others believed so as well. That was one reason her father cast her out. He could not turn a profit by offering her tainted hand in marriage.

Jordie wiped the tears from the edges of her eyes.

Boden came back inside with his puppy and a freshly washed face. He sat down at the table and began munching on a roll. She smiled at him as she brought him some venison stew steaming in a bowl.

"Mum," he began, "why is my grandpa standing in our yard?"

Jordie looked at him confused but then ordered him to stay inside and finish eating his supper while she went outside to investigate. She wrapped herself in a scarf and grabbed her hatchet. Jordie took a look at Ranger, but he stood still by Boden. Jordie nodded to her four-legged companion as she headed out in the crisp winter air.

Her father, as Boden said, waited outside.

Jordie gazed warily at him. Had he come here to take her in or to make amends? His chestnut hair was graying at the sides. His dark eyes flashed with anger behind a brow creased with contempt. She gripped her hatchet.

Robert grinned. "Expecting something hostile, daughter?"

"That depends on the manner of your visit, Father."

"You have grown bold, Jordie."

"Eight years on your own does that to you."

Robert's face went sour. "I summon you to the keep. A future husband awaits you."

Jordie laughed openly. "Really? You came here on a personal errand?"

"I won't stand for your lip, girl!" Robert yelled.

"Oh, aye, you will," she scowled, striding towards her father, feeling the anger rise up in her.

She felt as though she could take on the Goddess herself. She threw her shoulders back and stared up at her father. A calm coldness washed over her as she said, "You banished me to this cottage, away from the castle and the clan. You haven't spoken to me in almost eight years, and now you demand my presence?" She spat as his feet. "I think not!"

"You will do as you are told!"

They stood nose to nose.

Robert's nostrils flared as his cheeks heated red. However, she was calm, gently feeding herself an ever-flowing stream of resentment that had built itself over the years of complete solitude. She faced him as long as she dared. Then she took a step towards him, pushing him back towards the trail. Her blazing eyes never left his.

"No," she said flatly.

"You are to be married and get yourself out of my presence and life for good," he gritted out.

"I already am out of your life and presence. It was you who came to see me!"

"I will break you, and you know I will! You will do as I say or else!"

She laughed coldly. "Then I suggest you just try. Try to break me! I dare you!" And she walked back into her home.

"Stop this instant, young lady! The men I have asked to come for your hand surround your home. Is this how you wish for them to see you?"

Jordie spun around to glare at her father a final time. "I don't care! To the abyss with you." She opened the door, saying, "*Try* and break me!"

"Damn you to the abyss, Jordie!"

"Equal measure, Father," she said and slammed the door shut.

She let out a sigh of frustration. What she really wanted to do was scream, or to go hunting, but she had a small pair of gray eyes watching her every move. There was an example to be set. She looked over at Boden. He sat at the table swirling his stew with a spoon, focused and quiet.

Finally, he looked up. "Was that man truly my grandfather?"

"Aye," she answered.

"Was he always that mean?"

"Nay, time and hatred do that to a person," she said, stroking his head.

"Why does he hate you so much, Mum? That can't be right."

"Sometimes people make choices that cause the other person to view them as a lesser person," she said. "In this case, I had you as an unmarried woman. Robert cannot forgive me for that." She bent down to take his sweet face in her calloused hands. "But you know what?"

"What?"

"I would gladly have you a million times over than have your grandpa in my life."

Boden smiled. "I love you!" he said, wrapping his arms around her neck.

"I love you with every beat of my heart, always and forever," she said, hugging him fiercely. "Don't you ever forget that."

"I won't."

She hugged him long and hard until he began pulling away, saying that she was squishing the life out of him. She told him to go get ready for bed, which he did. Soon he was tucked in bed up in the loft with his two kittens, Grouch and Rusty, along with his new puppy, Merle. Boden and his animal friends soon fell asleep after that long cold day.

Jordie went down the ladder and outside the cottage door, shutting it as gently as the creaking hinges would allow. Once outside, she sat on a stump and cried. Everything from the day finally overwhelmed her, from what Harrison Fisher had said, down to the argument with her father, and the simple stupid things in between.

"Chin up, girl," she said to herself, "Things will get better. Tomorrow is a new day." She dried her eyes on the hem of her sleeve. "Tomorrow is new."

CHAPTER SEVEN

Tomorrow was indeed a new day, and it dawned with a clamorous pounding on her cottage door, right as the sun began its fiery ascent in the sky. She pulled herself out of bed and answered the door in a tunic.

"What do you want?" she asked, yawning and rubbing her eyes.

Ten men stared stonily down at her.

"Well, what are you here for? Obviously, my father sent you, so get to the damned point."

"You are summoned," one said.

"Not going," she responded, shutting the door in his face but his boot caught in the door.

"Aye, you are going, Jordie," he said, his tone firm. "You are going or else."

Jordie laughed in their faces. "No," she said crossing her arms. "I will take the 'or else' part then."

"Bound and gagged in front of your son? Have it your way. We have our orders, and they will be fulfilled, with or without your say-so."

She knew she couldn't take ten men on, whether it be verbally or physically. She would lose. Then she *would be* bound and gagged in front of her son. That was not something she wanted him to see. Angry with her defeat, she rolled her eyes and stepped to the side of the door.

"My son is still sleeping. Can it wait until he wakes up?"

"We can wait," he said, entering her home. "But you *are* going."

She nodded. "You men want tea?" she asked as politely as she could through thinned lips and a fake smile.

They grunted and came inside.

The commotion must have woken her son, for he poked his head over the side of the loft, watching the scene below.

"Mum?" he asked sleepily, rubbing his eyes.

"Get dressed, Boden. We are summoned to the castle."

She walked into her chamber, shutting the door behind her, and put on a fresher tunic and better trews. It took her only a moment to dress before she opened the door to ten men staring at her disapprovingly. She snorted at them all, rolling her eyes, and walking over to the kettle to boil water for tea.

A tense silence settled in the small cottage. Boden came down from the loft with all his animals. Jordie kissed his soft, sleepy head, handing him a roll and a clay mug of cow's milk.

"Take your pets outside to potty. Then get the eggs, all right?"

"Aye, Mum."

She didn't want Boden in here if and when they decided to speak to her. She knew it would take her son at least fifteen minutes if not more to complete his task. These men were here for her and her son, to drag them to the castle to have a different future doled out to them.

As Jordie served them tea and rolls, she didn't say a word. She didn't look them in the eye but stood by the counter, staring at the door with a determined gaze. Finally, one of them coughed before addressing her.

"Woman, are you not going to ask why you are summoned?"

"I do not care."

"Your son needs a father."

"Do *not* tell me what *my* son needs," she growled.

The warrior glared back at her but said nothing.

She was thankful that no one spoke to her after that. The anger she kept locked away was boiling, raging, about to spill over. She had seven years of peace. Seven years of living every day happily without being ordered around or talked down to like a nobody. If she wanted to speak to someone, she did so, but now she was being forced into a situation and her son was, again, the helpless victim.

Needless to say, she didn't like it.

Boden came back inside the cottage, beaming happily, while staring at the thing cupped between his hands. The handle of the basket of eggs swung on his right arm. Jordie bent down to his level as he held out his cupped hands.

"What do you have?" Jordie asked.

"A big ol' frog!" Boden replied, opening his hands.

The wet creature leaped out of his hands and onto her dark red hair. Boden burst out laughing uncontrollably. Jordie grabbed the frog and took the basket of eggs from her son.

"He needs to go back outside," she said, handing him the frog.

"But I want to keep him, please, Mum."

"Babe," she said, putting her hands around his, "he has a family to get back to. Do you want to take him away from that?"

"Nay, I don't."

She kissed his forehead, "Put him back, sweetling. We have to go to the castle with these men."

"Are you in trouble?"

"Nay, honey. I am going to talk to some people."

Boden nodded.

Jordie turned to the men. "Well, let's get going. I have a home and animals to get back to."

The men tramped their way out the door. She motioned for Ranger to stay in the yard. Jordie held onto her son's shoulder and whispered for him to stick close to her.

Together they made their way through the twisting path to the castle. Five men walked in front of her while the other five went behind. Truly, her father wasn't joking when he said he would break her.

They entered the tall arch-way into the dining hall. The tables and benches were empty. The candles on the wall were lit. The black speckled stone floor was swept clean. Fresh cloths waited on the tables. There was a grand fir tree on the main floor, all decorated in paper rings and different shapes, standing at least fourteen feet high and placed exactly in the middle between the two spiral staircases behind the royal high table.

The men walked her up the stairs to the right and stopped at the second door. One of the men opened the door, motioning for her and her son to enter.

"King Duvoir ordered you a bath to rinse off that stench," he said.

"I wish he could order you a new face," Jordie replied. "Mayhap then even pigs could withstand you."

The man slammed the door shut, leaving her and her son in her old chamber. There was only one bed and a small pallet on the floor. Boden walked over to it curiously.

"What is this on the floor, Mum?"

"It's for me, honey. They got you a bed."

As the man had said, there was a hot bath. It was next to the fireplace with a fire already roaring in the hearth. There was a small table next to the tub with perfumes, soaps, and cloths. In eight years, she hadn't smelled anything nice, taken a hot bath, or had anything of luxury. She uncorked a bottle of jasmine scent. Jordie inhaled it deeply, closing her eyes, savoring the sweet fragrance.

A knock came at the door. She waved at her son not to answer it as she approached the door, hand on her hatchet.

A young woman stood before her. "Hello, miss, I came on behalf of the queen. She wants to know if Boden would care to train with the other young squires this afternoon."

Jordie looked over at her son. "Would you like to go while I handle business?"

She knew that Boden was not to be present for whatever came next. It would be in his best interest to go play and not be around to overhear anything that might be said.

Boden slipped his hand into hers. "Is it all right?"

"You don't have to if you don't want to."

"Miss, there are four other boys his age here from his school," the servant girl said.

"Reid and Jacob are there?" Boden asked the woman.

"Aye," she said, bending down slightly, "along with Norman and Harry."

"May I go play?"

Jordie nodded and kissed her son. "Stay safe," she replied handing him one of her hatchets, "and protect yourself. If something happens, go to our place, all right?"

Boden hugged his mom.

"Nothing will happen, miss," the servant replied.

"It's Jordie," she told her, annoyed, and then leaned over say, "and it had better not."

"My name is Brietta. Your father says the men who will interview you to be their potential wife are in the room across the hall, when you are freshened."

"Interview?"

"Yes, Jordie."

The princess, slender and powerful, bent down to hug her son. "Have fun with your friends, and know that I love you."

"I love you too, Mum."

Boden left with the serving woman.

Jordie shut the chamber door and locked it. She turned towards her hot bath, looking at it with a mixture of longing and vexation. She couldn't properly remember the last time when she had a nice hot bath with soaps and perfumes. Obviously, her parents wanted her to make a good first impression. Too bad. She had other plans.

Jordie slipped off her clothes, getting into the nice, soothing hot water. She added a little jasmine scent. Then decided to dump the whole bottle in the water. Allowing the fragrance to relax her, Jordie laid her head back, enjoying it all, for it very well could be the last time she had such a luxury. And if it were the last time, she was going to make the best of it.

After soaking for a bit, she scrubbed her dark hair twice and washed herself all over. Slowly she got out of the tub. Her limbs were like pudding, wobbly and weak.

Jordie walked over to the vanity naked, looking at herself in the polished mirror. She hadn't seen her reflection in years. Her image had changed. She remembered the vivacious young girl, always smiling, happy, and carefree. A girl who loved life with a colorful flare and a pure, trusting soul.

But now in front of her stood a woman. Her skin was tanned and a scowl creased her brow. Her eyes weren't the cheery golden amber they used to be but instead were a hint darker. She had uneven tan lines on her skin, while her eyes popped with the contrast. Womanly curves embraced her body. Stretch marks from having her son were still visible, and slightly purple.

As she looked at herself, an idea began to form in her mind. A gutsy, immodest idea that was clever and a little stupid. She knew she had to do this for her son. Her father would not be in attendance at this meeting, she was sure of it, for he could not stand her presence. So, she would do this—anything for her son, to get their quiet, simple life back, and to get this over with as quickly as possible.

Jordie ran the brush through her wet red hair, then grabbed her cloak. She threw it on and walked to the chamber across the hallway, where all of the men would be.

Her father wanted these men to see her, just to be rid of her. These men had come to interview her, to see what she was like. To see if she was the trash she was reputed to be.

Interview, my butt, she thought.

She opened the door and peered in with hard, calculating eyes. But no one was in the room, just a bed chamber with a sword and a few other things on top of the quilt. She went to the next door, to the left, and opened it.

And inside she found what awaited her.

JORDIE IN CHARGE

CHAPTER EIGHT

She opened the next door to the room with her future awaiting inside. Her pulse wasn't pounding. Her skin wasn't clammy or sweaty. She was resolute and unafraid of what would happen next, for she knew only the strongest man of empathy would have her. Only the most understanding of men would find the kindness to stand beside her. And if one of these men had it, great. And if not, that was also fine with her. In either case, Corwaithe would walk beside her, as she always had.

All the men had their backs to her. By their garb she could see that all eight men hailed from eight different clans, including one from Drensent in Euainley. A lone stool stood in a semicircle of men. The stool where she would sit and be viewed as a potential wife. The men all had on a varying degree of clothing; each one had a different look. Some sat in the chairs tall and proud, while others were stooped and arrogant, scowling at the floor. Impatiently waiting for her.

Jordie smiled to herself as she removed her cloak, putting it on the peg by the door. She walked naked to her stool in the middle of the ring of men. Some of the men looked up in surprise while others averted their eyes in disgust at her shocking appearance.

"Get some clothes on, lass," a blue-eyed man said.

"I would have you see me as I am," Jordie replied, wriggling her bare bottom on the seat. "Let us all introduce ourselves. You all know who I am, but I have yet to learn your names. So, let's get started. I have a home and livestock to get back to."

"I be Kade Bonteva from Rowanoake," said the man who spoke first. "Why do ye behave so?"

Jordie raised a brow. "Behave as what, my lord?"

"Behave as a harlot?"

Her plan was working already. Jordie looked down at her feet to hide her smile.

"I am a harlot for being naked?" she asked. "I figured you would like to see what you are getting yourself into. So, if I am a harlot in your eyes, then so be it. I couldn't give a shit."

"Honestly," he sputtered, "this is who ye wish ta be seen as? Yer naked in front o' eight men, lass. Have some decency."

"You are only getting mad because you are offended by my honesty. I would think, as a respectable man, that you would appreciate my openness. You're going to judge me in one way or another. So, judge all of me," she chortled. "Have at it."

"I'm done," Kade replied getting up. "The rest o' ye have at it," he said as he reached the door and slammed it shut behind him.

One down.

The rest of the men went around introducing themselves—Justin Hernan from Hernan Castle, Findley MacKerwin from Earnswey, Brock Vorteva from Evermoor, Ryder Wendren from Wendren, Simon MacFarlane from Brocleigh, Brett Flornistas from Flowermoss, and finally, Locryn Mercendi from Drensent in Euainley.

Some were scarred in the face and arms, while others showed no signs of having lived a rugged life. They were all so different, all living various lifestyles, while she lived only one as the world passed her by.

"Well, don't be shy. Since I am being evaluated like a sheep for barter, you might as well put your gaping mouths to use and find out what you're in for," she told them. "The only reason I am here is because my father threatened me, so come on. Daylight is burning."

"Fair enough," spoke Brett. "How did ye come ta have a bairn so young?"

"I was young and in love."

"And where be this man now?" he asked.

"I do not know."

"Does Boden ken who his father be?"

"I have told my son about his father."

Brett raised an eyebrow. "And?"

Jordie rolled her eyes before she elaborated. "Boden thinks it's his fault that he doesn't have a father."

"And what did ye tell him lass?" Brett asked.

"That it is no one's fault but his father's."

69

"That be no' right," Brett spoke up, standing with conviction. "It be yer fault fer bein' a whore."

"I loved a man and in that love, I gave him my all. I have no shame in that. Corwaithe blessed me with two gifts, a wonderful son and a more powerful sense of self than what I knew of myself back then. If there is to be fault placed, then I place it on his father, Lane Flashew, for walking away from these gifts. I blame Lane for not wanting to be a part of the special life that I bore into this world. I cannot make someone love me. I cannot make someone stay."

Brett looked at her like she was set aflame. Brett's mousey brown hair frizzed all over his head as his pudgy face turned purple, and lips curled in a sneer. He stomped out the door.

Two down, six to go, she thought.

"So ye truly dinnae have shame in sleepin' with a man oot o' marriage?" Justin Hernan spoke, breaking the intense silence once again.

He was a handsome man, with a thick light brown beard and dark brown hair braided back down his head like a woman's. His amber eyes pierced hers.

"Nay, my lord, I do not," Jordie responded, straightening herself proudly on the chair.

"Then yer no' verra intelligent, be ye?" he said, quirking his brow.

"I followed my heart. I loved him with everything that I was. Nay, at that time I was not smart. I was foolish. But I am wiser now."

"Yer still no' smart, milady."

"No one is ever going to be fully intelligent and all-knowing," she countered.

"Nay, milady, ye misunderstood, yer *still* no' smart," Justin smirked and a few others laughed as well.

"Well, as Corwaithe so deems. Some she blesses with beauty, others intellect. You may have one, but the other remains to be seen."

A few of the other men chuckled at that, but she continued on, "I bear no shame in my son or myself. I have no shame that I loved someone. I grew as a person and a mother. And I have come to realize that I am only going to attract what I think I am worth. At the time, I didn't have a good opinion of myself, but now I want someone who can love me as I am and who will be my equal. It's clear as Corwaithe's glass, that person is not you."

More men snickered while Justin left the room, slamming the door behind him.

Three down! she laughed to herself.

As she glanced around the room, she wondered if anyone here would be brave enough to take on her and her son. To love them, to accept them, to make them a part of their life and clan. She seriously doubted it. Her father ordered her to marry or, more or less, ordered one of these men to marry her. Hopefully one of them was worth a damn. Although she seriously doubted it.

Minutes ticked by as no one spoke. They all sat with their arms crossed or in their laps, staring at her like she was something foreign that came out of a forest. She didn't mind in the least. They were assessing her and she was doing the same.

One more got up and left. Then another followed. Brock Vorteva and Ryder Wendren.

This is easier than felling broeshilak with an arrow!

Findley MacKerwin had spiky red hair and intense green eyes. He had a few scars on his hands and one thick scar that ran from his ear to his chin. He was a well-built man at about medium height, just a little taller than she.

Simon MacFarlane, from what she remembered in her lessons, was the adopted son of Laird Brogan MacFarlane to the west. Brogan was a fierce fighting man and well respected, as were his sons. Simon had no scars upon his person, but was a towering man, with thick, cropped black hair and eyes so dark they appeared black.

Now, Locryn Mercendi was different by far. He wasn't tall like the others; in fact, he was on the shorter side but his bulk made up for his lack of height. His body was so wide and thick that his muscles bulged against his tunic. She knew his father, Conner Mercendi, to be a well-built man, but this man before her was impressive. He had these startling blue eyes that appeared almost translucent under a thick cropping of strawberry blond hair.

All of these men looked powerful in their own way. They all came from well-known families, warriors who made their name on the field of battle. She couldn't compete with that. Her family was known for having birthed only girls. The only other clan that had girls was Clouneder. And here she was, the second eldest out of seven, being displayed like a cow.

Jordie never thought herself pretty. She had long, dark, cherry red hair and amber eyes like a wheat field in spring, except that field was now muddy in the middle of winter. She was tall but not overly so. She still had a small roll of belly fat from having her son years before. Jordie knew her body was off-putting. She wasn't thin. She had thick, wide thighs and hips, with a good-sized handful of breasts. She was what her mother had once called a voluptuous woman.

So, there she sat, perched on her stool, looking defiantly at the three men who were still there, interested in her hand. It was ridiculous. What was she supposed to do, spill her guts and cross her fingers that someone would actually like her enough to take her home?

Jordie got tired of the silence. "So, what next? What do you all plan on asking me?"

"Anythin' ye care ta tell *us* lass," Simon told her with his arms crossed.

"Why did you all come here?" she asked, ignoring him.

Findley leaned forward in his seat. "The money yer father be givin' fer yer hand."

Jordie looked shocked. "You want to marry a woman for money?"

"Aye," Simon added. "It be quite a sum ta be rid o' ye."

Jordie felt as if the wind got knocked out of her. Eight years of peace, then her simple perfect life interrupted, all over coin. And these idiots thought her father was actually going to pay them a substantial sum!

Jordie just laughed. "Fools! You've wasted your time."

"Ye bore a son," Simon said, none too thrilled with being laughed at. "Ye can bear more."

Jordie sobered.

Of course, these men wanted sons, she thought to herself. *It's one of the reasons they have women around. Not because they actually love them.*

She stared Simon down, silently praying that he wouldn't be the last man standing. She glanced over at Locryn. He leaned back in his seat, legs spread wide and arms crossed. Findley sat forward, shaking his head as if at his own private joke. Simon stood and paced the room.

"Care ta tell us anythin' more, lass?" Simon asked again.

"Like what? Are you wanting me to tell you everything about myself?"

"If that be what ye wish ta say."

"You have to earn the right to get to know me."

"Actually, I *do* have the right ta ken. That be why yer father brought us here."

Jordie snorted. "Do you see me as your equal or your inferior?"

"Be ye turnin' the tables, lass? Fer the last time I noticed, we men were ta question ye."

74

Jordie could feel a headache coming on. "I see now. You see me as an inferior woman with a decisive opinion."

"Somethin' like that."

"Then tell me, Oh Superior, where did women come from?"

His eyes narrowed and he stopped in front of her. "From Corwaithe, created by her oot o' the skin o' man. Everyone kens why as well."

"Obviously, *you* don't."

Simon crossed his arms over his chest. "Do tell, since ye most likely will anyway."

"You can count on that. Corwaithe made women not out of the ashes of fire as she did man, to be strong, protective, and brash. She did not make women from different clay than she did man. She made women out of the skin of man, to cover the wounds they may suffer, to heal their outsides but protect their heart. To be a man's first protectant."

Simon snorted. "Ye think so, lass?"

"Women were made for men, not the other way around."

"What be ye sayin'?"

"Women can survive without men. Look at me for example. I *am* alone, living on the outskirts of my own clan as an outcast from everyone, raising a son by myself, doing chores like a man, without a man."

"Ye think so, lass?"

"I have been doing it by myself, Lord MacFarlane," she said crossing her arms, "for seven years, almost eight. I have provided enough for us, done everything in my power to thrive. I do not need a man to make me whole."

"Ye sure be a cynical wee lass," Locryn Mercendi said contributing to the conversation.

"Nay, my lord, I be realistic," she responded.

"And what be real ta ye, lass?" Locryn asked.

Jordie glared at him. Then she hung her head, looking down at her feet.

Everything to her was real. Being alone was real. Raising a young man by herself was real. Raising a young man on her own while being an outcast was real. How can life not be real? How can this life she had been living on her own not be real? And what the abyss kind of question was that?

What man would want this? What man would want her?

Tears sprung to her eyes, but she looked up at the men boldly. "Everything is real. Being alone is real. Doing everything on my own because I am an outcast is real. And yet you three are the only ones who remain to view me as a piece of meat at a market because we were all in some way forced into this."

There was a long, tense silence. She didn't look at them. She realized now she was trapped. This was all a setup. Her father would not let her live here for much longer as an unmarried woman. He would find a way to get rid of her and this was it.

And when they said nothing, she raised her head and stared at each of them angrily.

"It's ridiculous, you know," she said as tears streamed down her face. "It should be me asking you stupid questions to get a feel for your character. It should be me seeing if you happen to fit into our lives because after all, Boden and I are a package. So, you just sit here on your asses contemplating which of you is brave enough to have us in your lives. Just know, I don't want this, but I do want what is best for my son. So, if I must marry to make his life better, then I will do it for him."

She finished her speech and stood up off her stool. Naked, she strode over to the wall where her cloak hung up and draped it around herself. She stared back at them, disgusted, angry, lonely, and empty. There was so much she wanted to say and yet she didn't want to give them the satisfaction.

"Jordie," Simon called. "Stop."

"No."

"Do as ye be told, lass," he said striding over to her.

"No!"

Simon reached up to strike her, but her hand caught his fist. Locryn's chair screeched and fell backward. His face was grim, his eyes icy. Findley also got out of his chair, waiting to see what was going to happen next.

"Damn you!" she seethed at Simon, shoving his fist aside.

"Damn me?" Simon said scowling. "Be ye really goin' there, lass? I will spank yer bare arse!"

"Aye, damn you!" she challenged. "And I bloody well dare you to do it! And for Corwaithe's sake, my bloody name is Jordie! You have no idea what it is like walking in my shoes, yet you act like you know what is honorable and true. Like you have courage and accountability. Yet I see none of it. If what that were true, then you all would look past what I did and take me and my son on, but instead I get this," she said, motioning to the chairs and the room.

"If ye were honorable, then ye wouldn't have bedded another man befer marriage," Simon answered.

"So, it's all right for a man to impregnate whomever he chooses, be it a bar wench or a roadside harlot, but for a woman to love a man and get left stranded in the woods while pregnant, give birth and be alone, well, shit, she's a whore."

"Really, Jordie?" he asked sarcastically.

"Really, Simon? Get lost, get gone, go away, don't come back, and all the other memorable farewells I could tell you!"

"At least yer accountable fer yer shit!"

"Aye, at least I am!"

"Fine," he said, exasperated, "I will say it—yer a whore!" He walked past her and out the door.

Jordie sunk to the floor, crying.

There was a short silence in the room before Findley walked over to her. She forgot they were still there. But she was done. She didn't want anything to do with the rest of them. She just wanted to be left alone.

"Jordie," Findley said quietly, kneeling down to her, "I have ken about ye fer years from yer sisters and family. And yet, from what I see, yer an honest and true lass and I admire that. But yer no' fer me. It's no' yer son or yer past or anythin' the like. I really admire yer sister Kathleen and I want ta marry her. Do ye think ye can help me?"

Jordie laughed. Softly at first then it slowly rose to an uproariously snort-filled laugh. Out of everything, she didn't expect a man to ask for her advice on what to do.

"Sorry," she said, at the bemused look on Findley's face, "that was a twist I wasn't expecting. Aye, Findley, I can help you. Go to our mother and petition for her hand first, then go to my father. He will say no but my mother always gets her way. It might take a few days for an answer, but Mother gets what she wants. At least that was how it was before when Maggie's husband wanted her hand."

Findley chuckled, "Yer a good woman, Jordie."

She almost rolled her eyes at that but nodded instead.

With a bow, Findley too walked out the door. She knew he was going to find her younger sister. It was about time they did something with their infatuation. It was all the villagers talked about lately. Findley would be good for Kathleen and she was excited for them both. Even if she hadn't seen any of her sisters in a very long time.

Out of all her sisters, Jordie had always been the carefree one—that is, until Lane. She was serious about him, once upon a time. Changed forever the day the bastard left.

Her life changed forever that day. And there was no going back.

She sat there on the floor for a moment longer. She knew she had to get back to her son back down to the cottage in the woods. If anybody was worth a damn, they could find her there.

Jordie sighed.

Resolutely she got up, dusted off her cloak, and put her hand on the doorknob to turn the handle. But she couldn't. She just couldn't turn that knob just yet.

"What am I going to tell Boden?" she said, leaning her head against the doorframe. "Shit!"

He would be waiting to find out what happened and if he would have a new father. He was so excited about it, she could tell. Boden yearned for a father. Her son deserved so much more than she could ever give him. She couldn't teach him everything, like how to fight, or how to build a home, or even how to fish like a man could. Even if she tried, it wouldn't be the same. Men spoke their own language, and often not in words.

Tears blurred her vision. She hadn't cried like this in years. "I'm such a failure," she whispered. She never meant to fail her son, but she felt so hopeless. Boden longed for a father and she couldn't give that to him.

Locryn cleared his throat. "Jordie," he said in a deep voice that filled the room, "yer no' a failure, lass."

Surprised, Jordie blinked the tears away. "Then what would you call me?"

80

Locryn smirked. "Interestingly clever."

"How am I clever, my lord?"

He came up behind her, took her hand, and twirled her around. Silently, he wiped the last of the trickling tears away with his thumb.

"Yer clever because ye wheedled down the men ye knew could no' handle ye, lass. We were supposed ta test ye, but ye tested us instead. That be clever, smart, and verra . . . immodest," he chuckled.

His laugh was just as deep as his voice. He was an intimidating man from this close-up view. His nose was tweaked, more than likely broken once or twice before. He had a wide scar that came across his left shoulder and up his neck. He noticed her glance.

She didn't like him being this close to her, mere inches away. He smelled of fir trees in winter time. She lightly touched his large chest, trying to get him to back up.

Her eyes darted to the scar and remained fixated. So badly she wanted to touch it, but she refrained. His muscles bulged out of the tunic. His scent reminded her of memories that she kept hidden away. Her fingers ached to be on his skin, but she closed her fist and looked up at the Drensent lord.

"I am sorry, my lord, for staring, but may I ask what happened?" she asked, gazing into his clear blue eyes.

"Battle with a rabble group from Orthilio. They took a lass from our clan."

She raised an eyebrow but did not ask further. If what he said was true, then he was an honorable man. And if not, then he was just another snake in the grass.

So instead she changed the subject. "And where does this leave us, since you are the last man standing here?"

He leaned in closer and instinctually she backed up, her body against the door. His head came down close to hers. His breath on hers as his head came sideways towards her cheek. Jordie turned away as her body tingled from being so near this man, suddenly aware of how very naked she was under her cloak.

His blue eyes glimmered with a roguish smile.

"It means ye and Boden be mine, lass," he grinned, and planted a kiss on her lips.

CHAPTER NINE

She shoved him away from her and grabbed at the door, but he spun her around. Jordie glared at him. Haughtily she drew herself up, glaring at him with her fierce amber eyes.

His?

His!

After that inappropriate, uncalled for, unasked for kiss? He was a proud man, almost too proud, looking down at her like that.

Locryn had one hand holding onto her waist and the other behind her head. If he was planning on kissing someone again, she wished he would just kiss himself. Jordie wriggled out of his grasp and reached for the door. She had enough of men for one day.

"Good day, my lord," she said.

Locryn smirked, "Dinna ye want ta pick oot the day ye want ta marry?"

She snorted. "I am not marrying anyone."

"Aye, ye be no' marryin' *anyone*, lass, ye be marryin' me."

Jordie put her hands over her face, exasperated. "You don't understand."

Locryn took her small hands in his. "Then help me understand."

Jordie jerked away and walked out the door. She headed straight for her old room across the hall to get dressed. She yanked open the door and looked for her clothes. They were folded neatly on the vanity. With a rush of panic, she began dressing. She had to get out of here and back to her home with her son.

Help me understand, he had told her.

Jordie shook her head.

No man was that kind. No man wanted to get to know her, to care about her that much to go that far. If he was truly that sincere, then he was an oddity of a man. She dropped the cloak on the floor and pulled on her trews. Then she got on her boots, making sure her knives were still tucked away. Her tunic came on next and she tied it all up with a belt and secured her ever-faithful hatchet. When she turned around to leave, Locryn was standing in the doorway.

There was a dark scowl on his face, so she scowled back.

"There are worse things in the world than me wearing men's clothing."

He crossed his massive arms, his bulk hogging all the doorframe. "That no' be why I be scowlin', lass."

She put her hands on her hips. "I have a name and it's Jordie."

Locryn chuckled, "All right, Dee."

Her face burned with anger. "Don't you *ever* call me that," she said her voice rising in fury. "My name is Jordie, not *Dee*, not *lass*, Jordie!"

Locryn held up his hands placatingly as she strode past him.

•••••

He didn't know why she got so angry so quickly, but he was astute enough to surmise that her son's father had once called her that. He felt bad for this woman. She had endured everything for so long. All her hurt and anger had been locked away inside of her, only now welling up for the first time in years.

It was evident in the way she spoke to them all this morning. It was evident in the way she cried against the door-frame. The woman was collapsing in on herself because a person can only struggle for so long. And Jordie was well past that point.

Last night, her father dragged the men who were willing to see Jordie out to her cottage. He went out to her small ramshackle home along with Findley, Simon, and Kade. She was a bold wee thing, facing off against her father. He didn't care much for the person who helped create her and it was clear to him that neither did she.

He remembered her long red hair billowing in the crisp air as her voice rang out in the forest. He remembered her wee son going into the cottage and her coming out in a quiet burning fury.

Her home was small and even without looking inside, he knew she was very poor. In the lean-to shack, there was one cow and a nanny goat. She didn't even have a proper garden. She didn't even have a well. She had a home and a space for a beast next to it.

He remembered her standing in her yard, as a proud and strong woman, resilient and smart. And he remembered her from a few moments ago. Her love for her son was obvious. Her love for the boy seeped out of her skin like a warm kiss of bright sunshine. Jordie had so much love to give and that idiot Lane threw it all away, leaving Jordie guarded and bitter.

She was different from all the women he knew. True, they too got done what needed doing, but none were like Jordie. All this woman had was herself.

She was going to take some getting used to as she wouldn't want to rely on him for her needs. He would want to take care of her while she would want to take care of herself. His eyes softened to her; his brow grew less creased.

"Be ye willin' ta get ta ken me?" he asked after a moment.

Jordie turned around disgusted. "No!"

Locryn tried not to get frustrated with her. He decided to drop the subject for a while.

"Where did ye get that scar, Jordie?" he asked, breaking the scowl on her bonny face.

86

"What scar?"

"The scar on yer leg." He pointed to her right calf.

"A boar," she replied, shoving her way past him to go down the stairs.

•••••

She knew her son would be playing outside since it wasn't snowing or raining today. Jordie took the stairs down two at a time, trying to leave Locryn far behind. The men from earlier and a few others were sitting at the dining hall tables eating the nooning meal. She had to get her son, to get him back home and make him something to eat. She seriously doubted her parents would feed Boden.

The door creaked open as she slipped out.

Once outside, she looked up at the gray sky. It was cloudy yet not too bad, perfect for hunting their evening meal. The sun told her it was an hour or so past the nooning meal and her tummy rumbled. She hadn't eaten since yesterday.

She looked back over her shoulder at the last man standing. He had followed her and waited a few yards behind.

Jordie snorted.

His face softened towards her. Locryn was the type of man who would see a broeshilak with a broken leg and would want to fix it. But Jordie didn't need fixing. She needed love and respect.

She shook her head as she looked around the courtyard for her son.

There he was play-fighting with a wooden sword against another young boy, receiving instruction from none other than her own father. Jordie watched them for a while, impressed at how her son was doing. The ax she had given him earlier was still tucked into his belt. Jordie looked over at her mother, Cynthia, who sat in a chair watching her grandson square off with the young lad. Jordie walked over, scowling.

Her mother finally broke the silence. "Surely, you are not mad at your son?" she asked with a hint of disdain.

"Surely, I am not mad at my son," Jordie replied. "The only thing I would ever fault him for is if he got a woman with child and then just left her in the woods."

Her father came over to her, jaw set in stone. "How dare you talk to your mother in that fashion!"

"Curious. Last I heard, I was no longer yours nor hers."

Robert slapped her across the face. "Show some respect for your king."

Jordie laughed, provoking her red-faced father. "Come, Boden, that's enough fighting for the day."

She took her son's hand, but he looked at her with a mixture of sadness and anger. She knew the anger came from her being smacked. She would talk to him later about that, but for right now, she wanted to get him away from the people she once called parents.

"I hope a husband agreed to take you on," her father said. "I truly want you away from here."

"We shall see, Robert," she said, walking away.

"Apologize to your queen," Robert called.

Jordie turned around and dipped her head towards her mother.

"You're staying in the keep tonight," Robert called out again.

She kept walking with her son.

Like the abyss I am, she mumbled under her breath.

They walked in silence for a long time. Not even Boden said a word. When their home came into view, she let out a sigh of relief.

Her son went straight to his new puppy. The boy needed time all to himself to sort through his thoughts and what happened. What she really needed to do was tell him what would be happening now.

"Ye like the chaos, do ye no'?" Locryn's voice came from down the pathway.

Boden shrunk back behind Ranger as Locryn walked up to the cottage. Jordie huffed, irritated by the fact that everyone seemed to want something of her these days.

"I like being left alone," she snapped.

Locryn crossed his arms. "No lass likes bein' left alone."

"Well, this *lass* liked it just fine for the last seven years."

"Did ye really?"

CHAPTER TEN

She stood there before him, vulnerable and honest. Her amber eyes, sparkling with flecks of gold, pierced him with a deep sadness. Her full pink pouty lips called to him, even with the small bloody split in her lower lip.

Her father had no right to strike her. But she didn't even cry out or bat an eyelash. This woman was truly something fierce. After she left, he had had a few choice words with Robert. Locryn never cared for the man, but striking Jordie had been the final mark against him.

"So, this be where ye lived fer all these years?" Locryn asked coming up to her.

"Aye."

"All by yerself?" He took a kerchief out of his pocket, walked over to the water bucket, and dipped it in as they spoke.

"Aye."

"Then who got ye wood, food, clothin'?"

"I did," she said, crossing her arms. "I am not helpless, you know."

"Never said ye were, love," Locryn said and pressed the cloth on her bloody lip.

"Don't call me that," she said, pulling back.

Locryn chuckled. "All right, wee one." He moved closer and gently dabbed the cloth again.

She crossed her arms and kept still, forcing herself not to look into his brilliant eyes. He chuckled at her, finding her tantrum amusing. All the while, he stood there with his wet cloth pressed against her lip. Jordie hung her lead low and moved away from him.

He let her walk away, knowing this was all so new for her. She'd had no one around for so long, that this was going to take a lot of getting used to for her. And for him as well.

He was taking on a disrespected outcast daughter and her son. When he had asked the villagers about her the day before, they did not seem to mind her presence among them. In fact, most people felt sorry for her, but her hostile attitude kept them at bay.

Locryn looked over at her son, who was staring at him curiously.

"And who be this strappin' young man?" he asked.

The boy poked his head out from behind the big gray dog.

"My name is Boden, my lord."

Locryn approached the boy, ready to kneel down, but massive beast growled at him. So, he remained standing, giving the dog and boy some room. The dog seemed to smile at him as he backed away.

92

Boden petted the beast. "This is my dog, Ranger, and this pup is Merle."

"How auld be this fine dog?" Locryn asked, bending down to let the dog sniff his hand.

"I don't know. Mum had him before I was born and he talks to me sometimes," Boden replied petting the gray beast. "My lord?" Boden asked.

"Aye, Boden?"

"Why are you here?"

Locryn grinned. "I be goin' ta marry yer mum."

Boden scrunched his tiny face. "Can I keep my dogs?"

Locryn patted the old dog on the head and scratched him behind the ears. "Aye, Boden, ye can."

"Mum, does that mean you're really getting married?" her son asked, turning towards her.

"No," she told him.

"Aye, ye be marryin' me, lass."

"It's Jordie!"

"Well, yer still marryin' me."

"I don't even know you," she said.

"Because ye have no' even tried ta get ta ken me at all, ye stubborn woman."

"And if I got to know you, what would I find?"

Locryn blinked.

It all became clear to him. She was afraid of loving someone, of getting close to someone, only to be dismissed or turned away like before. To be left to fend for herself all over again. And in that protection, she was trying to save her son the heartache as well.

He felt for this woman. At seventeen years old, giving birth to a babe all alone in the forest and then fending for herself could not have been easy.

She walked past him to the woodshed, picking up a splitting mall and swinging it. He watched her split wood and stack it neatly beside the stump. Life, with or without him, would go on. She couldn't care less that he was here. Jordie was going to continue doing what she needed to regardless. She picked up the bundle of split wood, carrying it inside.

"What makes ye think I be the same?" he finally asked before she reached the door.

Jordie thought on that a moment before quietly replying, "I am afraid to find out."

Locryn took the firewood from her hands.

"Will ye give me a chance?"

She looked at him questioningly.

●●●●●

In truth, she was half-tempted to give him a chance. But another part of her was guarded. She didn't want her son to feel the same indescribable disappointment that she once had. And if this man were to disappoint, then they both would suffer from it.

Was Locryn different? He took bundle of wood out of her hands. He seemed to care about her and her son. He seemed determined to be here with her. Still, she was uncertain of him and men all together.

She shifted her feet uneasily, looking down at the ground. She glanced sideways at Boden who smiled back at her.

For you, my sweet boy, she thought.

Jordie, hands on her hips, stared hard at the lord before her. "Do I have to marry you?" she asked.

Locryn chuckled, "Aye, ye do."

"What if I don't like you after coming to know you?"

Locryn looked down at his feet, and sighed. "Well, I hope it does no' come ta that, but if it does, then I will let ye go."

Her dark brows furrowed curiously. "Just like that?"

"Aye, just like that."

She knew she didn't have to make him promise. He was a man of his word. That much she could gather straightaway. Her only concern was her son and how Boden would feel about this *new* father.

Would he hate him? Like him? Would Boden feel disappointed by him? Or would this time be different?

She didn't know. But there was only one way to find out, and that was to give this man a chance to prove himself. She had to at least try. For her son. Boden deserved as much.

Jordie shook her head.

She had been alone for so long, she had forgotten what it was like to trust. To love. But would Locryn be worthy of her trust? Would he be the man she needed him to be?

Nothing ventured, nothing gained, she reminded herself.

"I'll marry you then, my lord," Jordie conceded.

"Call me Locryn then, no' milaird," he told her.

"My what?" she asked, tilting her head.

"Milaird."

"My lord," Jordie corrected.

"Aye, milaird."

"Nay, my lord," she corrected again.

Locryn scowled. "Get used ta the language, lass, yer goin' ta be livin' with me and I told ye ta call me Locryn."

She wanted to giggle but refrained.

Then they both laughed. Boden peeked up at them with a grin on his small face. She couldn't help but grin back at her son. He was so full of life and innocence. This was a happy moment for her young man. He was finally getting something she longed to give him.

Boden whistled for his dogs to follow him into the house. Jordie followed behind her son. Locryn still stood by the woodshed, holding her bundle of wood. She waved for him to join them, and they all went in the house together.

•••••

Jordie held the door open for him.

It was as he assumed: a small cottage, barely enough room to fit his bulk through the door let alone inside. He stood one small step inside the house. To his left was a door. He could only assume it was to Jordie's bedroom. At his right stood a small table with four chairs. In front of him was the kitchen. Above it was a loft where Boden sat, staring down at him. Then there was a little room for two small cushioned chairs before the fireplace, wide enough for Jordie and her son.

The cozy house was just big enough for them both. It was very small but had a cozy feel. Jordie sat on top of the kitchen counter which was a slab of rough-hewn wood, made slightly smoother over time.

"And this has been yer home since he left ye here," he said, anger tinging his voice.

She nodded.

"Actually," a man's voice said by the kitchen table, "this is my home."

Jordie's mouth dropped open.

Boden smiled at the strange man.

He looked half-human, half-dog with dark skin and golden eyes. Hair covered his body in patches as he lounged at the kitchen table. He moved in front of Jordie, but she stepped around him, getting a good look at the shifter in front of her.

"Aramoren?" she questioned.

The man nodded. "The one and only."

Locryn's eyes widened and he became angry. This woman truly was a whore. He looked at her disgusted, backing away and heading towards the door. She was not a woman he wanted to take home to his mother or his people.

Aramoren snapped his fingers and the iron door handle locked and a large cushioned chair appeared. "Take a seat, my crazy-brained friend," the shape-shifter said, "and do it now, before any more wild, ignorant thoughts go rampaging through that little head of yours. I helped deliver her son and have watched over her. But I *never* wanted her in that fashion."

Jordie's mouth opened and closed a few times. "It was you, all those years ago?"

"Yes, it was," Aramoren nodded, leaning back in the kitchen chair with an arm sloped over the side.

"But why?" she stammered.

Aramoren tapped a finger to the side of his chin. "Well, you really didn't give me much of a choice as you were in *my* home."

"I didn't know," she exclaimed, interrupting the beast. "I thought Lane built it."

98

The shifter laughed. "Not at all, dear! He found it, and I sensed his intentions. I decided to play along and let you stay awhile because there was just something about you I admired. Like I said before, I find you interesting."

"How so?" she asked.

Aramoren looked at her, his yellow eyes beaming at her, "You're tenacious, in the most . . . foolhardy yet endearing way."

Aramoren leaned forward, gray wiry hair poking out down his back. A tail protruded just above his buttocks. Locryn tried to get out of his chair but he was bound to it. Jordie also wasn't moving a muscle. Aramoren leaped over to Boden who by now had come down from the loft.

"Little intruder," the shifting beast said, "you're going to have to learn to trust this man."

"Why?"

"He is all you're going to have, among other reasons," he said. "Tomorrow, I get my house back and you leave with Locryn."

Aramoren walked over to study him with a wolfish smile. His teeth came out over top of his bottom lip, adding to his canine features. Locryn hadn't gotten a good enough look at his face until this moment, but his furry features were oddly human. Yet even his ears were doggish.

Locryn stared at him for a long time, trying to deduce whether he was friend or foe. He tried to wriggle out of the chair but he couldn't seem to get away. Aramoren grinned.

"Not to worry, I never wanted her like that," the beast began. "If I had, she would have been mine. But yes, the answer to your question is he did leave her here. And she had not a clue about me. Well, maybe one clue. Be as it may. No one came back for her. No one helped her. Especially not I, as I was already letting her live in *my* home."

Aramoren snapped his fingers and Locryn fell forward. The pressure and release of the invisible bonds caused him to lurch. Locryn pounced out of his chair and stood in front of Jordie.

"What d'ye want, Aramoren?" Locryn said.

The dog man sat in the cushioned chair, his gray fur sticking out all over. "Simple. My house back."

Locryn perked an eyebrow. "That's it?"

"Yes."

Then Aramoren clapped his hands together. "So, you," he pointed to Locryn, "have a bone to pick with Robert. I have errands to run." Aramoren looked at Jordie. "I will not see you tomorrow," he said, "but Jordie, it's been exhausting having you as a guest, so ta-ta!" And with a snap of his fingers, he disappeared.

Locryn looked at Jordie, wondering if she knew all along. She shook her head at him, clearly bewildered by everything that just happened. Boden looked between them and shrugged.

Locryn was having a hard time believing that she lived with a shape-shifter for the last seven years. How could she not know? However, the shocked look on her face testified that everything the animal man had said was true.

"Did ye ken?" he ventured to ask.

Jordie shook her head. "No, I didn't," she said, pale as snow. "I thought he was my dog, Ranger."

"He talked to me a lot, Mama," Boden said, running up to her. "He said to keep it a secret."

Jordie looked horrified at Locryn, then her son. "He spoke to you?"

Boden nodded. "*Love will find that woman, but she will be too blinded to see it,*" he repeated. "He also whined a lot about wanting his house to himself."

Locryn cleared his throat. "Well. That was eventful."

"I did not see that coming," Jordie responded.

"D'ye mind if I took a look around?"

"Be my guest."

Careful not to knock into anything, he opened her bedroom door. The room was just big enough for a bed and a chest. There wasn't a fireplace. There wasn't a wardrobe filled with beautiful dresses or even a drawer for soft leather slippers. There was just a bed, a side table, and a small chest.

Locryn came out and shut the door a little harder than he should have. Jordie still sat on the countertop looking at him questioningly. She looked like a horse tamer, speculating on what the wild colt was going to do next. She was so guarded.

Up in his loft, Boden sat on a small bed with a kitten in his lap and his pup beside him. He too had a small chest of clothes. It angered Locryn that after all this time, no one cared enough to come check on them. To make certain they had enough to eat or drink, or even to make sure they had blankets to keep warm and enough split wood to put in the fire.

Locryn came down the stairs of the loft. In three short strides, he stood in the middle of her home, facing her as she sat rigidly on the countertop.

"What was the last thing ye remember yer father tellin' ye befer ye came here?"

•••••

Jordie watching this man tour her home. What did Aramoren mean by learning to trust Locryn? What did the animal man know that she did not? Could her heart ever trust another person again?

Locryn's chest heaved, breathing deeply, almost angrily. Throughout their brief exchanges, he did not leave. He listened to what she had to say. He seemed to genuinely care about her and her son enough to learn about her, to see where she lived and what her life was like.

Her head tilted to the side as she pondered his question.

It was a peculiar question but she wasn't about to lie to him. If they were going to be in this relationship, she wasn't going to start off by lying or holding back. Jordie looked at the floor. She remembered that day all too well, for every last word of what was said spread like a plague in her brain for days.

She cleared her throat. "You are a disappointment to me, your mother, your sisters, this family, our people, and my last name. You are a slut, a whore, a common bar wench that I had the unfortunate privilege of conceiving. Do not come back into this keep unless you are summoned."

Locryn turned red with anger. "Anythin' else, lass?"

Jordie could feel the shame of that day come welling back. The tears stung her eyes something fierce, and her body felt like it was shrinking in on itself. She blinked back tears while still staring at the wood floor, her whole body shaking.

Again, she cleared her throat. "From this moment forward, no one is allowed to talk to that woman. She is also allowed to live in Veiled Hills, but as an outsider to this clan. That was the very last thing he said before I left the castle for good."

Locryn left her home in a rage. Growling, he slammed the door behind him. She never knew a man, other than her father, to become so instantly angered. When he left, she quickly hopped down and bolted the door shut, not wanting to let the outside world back in.

Boden looked over the loft railing, confused.

"Some men protect women, babe," she said. "He is one of the few men who feels so strongly about it."

Boden nodded. "Will he come back?"

"I don't know, Bo."

Boden looked thoughtful for a moment. "I like him, Mum. We wouldn't have to be alone anymore."

Jordie couldn't keep the tears back at that. "I am so sorry."

She felt so guilty at the life her son had to lead because of her. Even though it wasn't her fault, Boden had to bear the shame of it at times. The only good was that he thrived at school and he had friends. She looked at her little boy, who was growing up faster than she liked and smiling down at her.

"I love you," he told her, jumping down from the loft, and ran to give her a hug.

She bent down and hugged him back. "I love you too," she said, sniffling back the tears.

CHAPTER ELEVEN

L ocryn stomped up the trail all the way back to the castle to grab the priest that would marry them. It would happen right now, tonight. He was going to get her and Boden out of here, away from the people who had hurt them both. This was going to happen right now, so he could take her back to his home and provide for her. She would never want for anything ever again.

He would give her heaps of food, dresses, luxuries—whatever she wanted, whenever she wanted it. He would shield her from harm—verbal or physical. He knew he could not always be there to guard her from everything, but he would stand by her and protect her in ways he knew he could.

He stopped under the portcullis and there sat the dog man, watching him, nodding with his head to continue forward. But Locryn didn't move.

Aramoren trotting forward, sitting beside him as he faced the castle.

"She is a good woman," the dog man said.

"No one protected her, no' even ye," he said.

Aramoren cocked his head. "Fair enough," he conceded. "Now pet my head, and don't move your mouth so much."

Locryn bent down, scratching the beast rather roughly behind the ear.

"Thanks," said Aramoren, wagging his tail. "But she learned to protect herself. Now you must help her to trust."

"And why should I trust ye and yer kind?"

Aramoren sniffed. "My kind, huh? Well, obviously you have heard of *my kind*, and since you have, then you should know we are sensory beings—telepathic, if your one-way mind can comprehend that."

"I understand just fine."

Aramoren's tongue lolled to the side as he tilted his head. "Wonderful," he said. "Oh, and some advice before you go."

"What?"

"Don't waste your time with Robert. The man is an idiot," the dog said, trotting forward. "*I don't want to go into the forest, waste of resources*. If only he truly knew what was in that forest. But no worries. Once all three of you leave, it will be better. For us all, especially me."

Locryn watched the dog gallop off into the night. He shook his head at the beast. Shifters were heard of, but rarely did anyone meet one. Now he understood why.

He turned back around again to gaze off at the treetops, wondering what Jordie was doing beyond that. He felt a pull towards this woman. Although he wasn't quite sure where it came from, he liked her nonetheless. She was different, smart, and capable, which was something that appealed to him immensely. She was so guarded yet so starving to be loved and for her to love someone.

When Locryn entered the castle, he found the king and queen sitting at the high table beneath the Winter Feasting Tree. They were elbow-deep into their wooden plates of food.

He walked past a table that was piled with food. Mutton, mashed potatoes and gravy, rolls, boiled carrots, and roasted green beans were on one end of the table. The other end had chocolate pudding, a cake, several different kinds of drinks. The middle of the table had roasted birds and a large groewindel dressed with stuffing and a different kind of gravy.

Jordie had not tasted food like this in years. This was something he wanted to give to her every day—a plethora of food. She was already so slender.

When he strode up to the merry monarchs, the gluttonous king never looked up at him. Robert licked his fingers that dripped with groewindel juice. Locryn did not greet the man; his rage prevented him from using manners. He stood over the man, fists clenched in ire.

"What is it you need, Mercendi?" Robert Duvoir asked, irritated that the man was just standing before him scowling.

"I have come ta ask ye a few things, laird," he said, trying to keep the disgust from his voice. "First, why did ye turn yer back on a young lass in her time o' need?"

Robert dropped his groewindel leg. "She had bed a man before getting married. That makes her a whore. And a whore is not allowed in my castle."

"She made a foolish choice, aye, but be that a reason ta cast her oot ferever?"

"Aye, that is *my* reason." He paused to take a drink of mulled wine. "Now. Is there anything else."

"Aye. Where be the priest?"

Robert almost choked as he took another drink. "You're serious about marrying her?"

"Aye. She be a good woman."

Robert slid a hand over his face, then sighed, laughing out loud. The people closest to the king stopped and looked at them. Locryn knew that Robert was happy to be rid of his daughter. It only caused him to become more incensed.

"About time *someone* wanted that woman," Robert said. "Did she bed you already?"

Locryn clenched and unclenched his fists, trying to compose himself. More than anything he wanted to punch the man off his chair. He didn't know how anyone could speak of their child in that manner.

His family had always respected the Veiled Hills clan, but after today, after what Robert said about his own daughter, Locryn's respect was gone. Aye, their clans would always be allies, but Locryn would never have contact with his man ever again, nor anyone from this castle.

"I would appreciate it if ye didna talk about me future wife in that manner."

Robert held up his hands placatingly, "All right. And I take it you are taking the bastard with you?"

"*Boden* be me son."

Robert rubbed his hands together. "Good, good! This calls for a celebration!" He clapped his hands and a serving woman came forward with more wine. "Drink with me, Mercendi."

"Just tell me where I can find the priest."

Robert chuckled. "Eager, are we? Well, he should be here in a moment."

Locryn grunted and walked away before his fist connected with the king's face.

He sat down at a lone table by himself. He tried to wrest control over his thoughts. It astonished him that a father could hold that much resentment against his own daughter.

How could anyone be that cruel ta a bonny wee lass? he wondered.

Locryn sat contemplating all the things that would change for Jordie when she became his wife. Findley MacKerwin, heir to Earnswey, joined him but he hardly noticed. The man sat quietly, drinking his ale. Findley was his best friend. His clan was an ally to Drensent, and he was younger by a few years, but the difference was hardly noticeable. They were as close as blood brothers. In fact, he was closer to Findley than he was with his own brother, Thomas.

Findley clapped a hand on his shoulder. "Ho, Locryn."

"Hello, me drunken friend," Locryn greeted him with a smile.

Findley belched loudly. "No' drunk . . . yet," he grinned. "Celebrate with me, good brother."

"Celebrate what?" Locryn asked.

A lovely woman who looked to be a relation to Jordie came over and sat beside Findley. She was smaller than Jordie was and had red hair and hazel eyes. The lass was bonny, with pale butter-cream skin. She must have been one of Jordie's sisters. The only difference was their hair and Jordie's sparkling eyes.

"Findley, I thought you were going to ask my mother about us," the woman spoke demurely.

Findley grinned triumphantly. "I already did, me wee love! I be waitin' fer an answer befer I ask yer father."

"This is wonderful, Findley!"

Findley hiccupped, "It be why I be celebratin', lass."

Locryn looked at the woman his cousin loved. "Do ye no' miss yer sister Jordie?"

Kathleen whipped her head around. "I was fifteen when she left," she said with a hint of sadness. "She was my confidant. I miss her at times, but it has been so long now that I doubt she misses me at all. She had changed so much as well over the years."

"Have ye ever asked her if she misses ye? Or made the time ta go see her and talk?"

Kathleen shook her head. "No, we are forbidden from speaking to her."

The woman returned her attentions to her very inebriated lover.

At every turn, Jordie was left to her own devices. It was incredible that she had thrived as well as she had. Locryn turned his head away from his friend, looking out the high windows to see that it was dark outside. He needed to get back to Jordie to make sure she was all right.

He pushed his chair out just as Findley fell off of his. Locryn rolled his eyes and told Kathleen to leave him. Findley wasn't a cooperative drunk. The woman stooped down, trying to talk to him, but Findley was curled up sleepily, grumbling for her to leave him alone.

Locryn picked up an empty wooden plate and loaded it with food. He knew it had to have been years since she had a good meal. Then he grabbed a torch off the wall and made his way out into the chilly night without the priest.

JORDIE IN CHARGE

CHAPTER TWELVE

It was dark out.

Darker than what she thought it would be.

Night came early, so she was thankful she went out hunting after Locryn left to go do whatever men do, which she assumed was eating, drinking, and consorting with willing women.

Jordie snorted, rolling her golden eyes.

At this time of year, she needed all of her attention on hunting for food, not handsome, well-muscled distractions. The last thing she wanted was a promiscuous husband. She didn't want a husband at all, but she knew that after today, she would have one.

Jordie cringed at the thought.

That night she and Boden had a filling meal of salted boiled potatoes and a rabbit that Boden had caught himself. They went out hunting together, just as they had done since he was a babe. Boden had become quite the little hunter.

Jordie knew she wouldn't stop hunting anytime soon, even if she was married to a lord or whatever his title happened to be. Kills meant food and food meant respect and people liked others when they filled their bellies. Jordie didn't want to rely on a man to provide for her. Although in truth, men were the most dependable beings. She could always depend on them *not* to be there when she needed them.

Boden, thankfully, went to sleep early. He was tired from the sword fighting and then from the hunt. She was grateful that he was learning the craft of swordplay but not too pleased that the training came from her father. But she put that aside as Boden lit up during their supper, recounting the day's triumphs.

Anything to see him smile.

They talked about what was to happen soon, with her proposed marriage to Locryn. From what Boden told her, he seemed pleased with the idea. Boden went so far as to say that he liked Locryn and hoped he'd stay.

At least I am doing something right, she thought.

Boden went to sleep early, giving her a long time to reflect on the events of the day. Here, all along, she had thought Ranger was a dog and he wasn't. He was a shifter, a man who could transform into one particular animal. Shifters were not common and most children grew up knowing about them but not understanding how to spot them. Cynthia had told her about them while her father called the legends hogwash.

And now she knew that the house she thought Lane had built her was all a lie. She wondered how he even came across such a dwelling. Then again, she didn't want to know. Her home was not her home. As the dog man pointed out, she was an invader.

114

Jordie wanted to cry at the thought of losing her beloved home.

"I have come to like your presence, oddly enough," Aramoren said from the doorway.

Jordie jumped. "Thanks," she replied awkwardly.

The dog man came to sit in the chair beside her, his tail wagging in the firelight. "Well, you have been an invader for the last seven years," he said smirking.

"Sorry." Jordie ducked her head.

"It's all right. What's seven years? We are, after all, immortal."

"Immortal?" Jordie asked, brows furrowed.

"We shifters live forever."

Jordie bobbed her head, staring at the fire. She didn't know what else to say to the person she thought was her companion. She felt like she had lost a best friend.

"Trust him," Aramoren said.

"What?"

Aramoren fixed a look on her that would freeze a deer in place. "Trust him," he said, getting out of his chair and heading for the door. "You are so stubborn. He will be here soon."

And then he was gone.

She sighed, staring into the fire once again.

Locryn was patient with her while she knew she made things difficult. She did so out of fear. She didn't want to be trapped, or let down. She didn't want the sting of abandonment to fall on her head again. And she didn't want Boden to bear it either.

I will try, she told herself looking at the loft, *I will try for my son. He will have to prove to me that he means to stay, to be a father to Boden. But I will try.*

Merle's ears perked. He barked, eyes intent on the door. Jordie pulled a knife out of her boot, anticipating a foe. She walked lithely over to the door, opening it slowly, knife at the ready.

Locryn Mercendi stood at her doorstep with a torch and a plate of food. She lowered her weapon, standing aside.

"I brought ye food," he said. His blue eyes twinkled as he handed her the plate.

He isn't as bad as I thought, she thought and waved him in.

Then she woke her son so he could have a bite to eat. Boden climbed down the ladder, eyes wide at all the food, and dug in.

"Thank you for this," Jordie said.

Locryn nodded, a small smile on his lips as he sat by the hearth watching her son eat his fill. "Yer welcome."

When Boden was done, he thanked Locryn, yawing all the while, and went to bed. He was back asleep within moments.

Jordie didn't know what to say or what to do. Aramoren said to trust him, but that task seemed impossible. Inside, her emotions were a jumble. On one hand, she wanted to open up to this kind man who was considerate enough to bring her food when he didn't have to. On the other, she wanted nothing to do with him because to her, all men were merely walking, waiting, future disappointments.

But she needed answers. She needed to know why he was like this. Why he was kind, why was he interested in her, why wouldn't he leave? She glanced over at him, sitting in the cushioned chair, staring at the dying embers of the fire.

"Why?" she finally asked. "Why did you come back and with food?"

"Do ye no' like mutton, lass?"

"I like mutton, yes. But why did you come back?"

Locryn glowered at her, "Yer ta be me wife."

She didn't like that answer.

She didn't like what he did. Her heart raced, and anxiety filled her faster than a raging river in springtime. Her hands went clammy and her feet twitched to run. Panic must have registered on her face because Locryn got up out of his seat and came towards her, taking her hands in his.

"It be all right, lass." His blue eyes looked so warm, so gentle.

Jordie shook her head. "Nay, it is not all right."

"Want ta talk about it?"

117

"Me to be your wife?" she asked, distressed but helpless under the gaze of his star-like eyes. "And you're not supposed to be this nice."

"I be no' supposed ta be nice?" Locryn asked, chuckling.

"Men are never that nice."

Locryn grabbed ahold of her hand, stroking the top of it gently with his thumb. "Ye canna go around refusin' ta eat an apple because two in the barrel be rotten. And ye be afraid ta get close. Yer afraid ta let go o' control."

Am I truly that easy to read? she asked herself.

"I don't even know you," she told him.

He rubbed the back of her hand. "Then get ta ken me, Jordie. Yer goin' ta have ta trust that I wilna leave ye. But first, eat. Befer it gets cold."

She broke away from his touch that felt too hot. She sat in the chair Boden previously occupied. Methodically, she ate what was left, as she was still hungry.

Get ta ken me, he told her.

But she was scared to get to know him. Getting to know him meant talking. Talking meant revealing things about herself, and when he discovered everything about her, would he then become bored with her or would he leave? Mayhap he would turn cruel and hit her. Nay, Locryn wouldn't do that.

Jordie sat down in the chair next to Locryn. "Care to talk with me tonight, so I can get to know you and you can get to know me?"

118

If he was making an effort, for her and her son, then she should as well. She had to try to make this work for them both. Mainly for Boden. He deserved a caring father. Locryn's one little gesture, even something as small as bringing food, was enough to turn the tide for now.

"Aye, I would like that, Jordie."

Jordie smiled, for the first time in a long time, at a man.

JORDIE IN CHARGE

CHAPTER THIRTEEN

She gave him a genuine smile.

Warmth, like sunshine, spread through his chest. She was so beautiful when she smiled. Her bright white teeth glowed almost silver against her sun-kissed skin in the dying light of the hearth. Her long, dark red hair was mussed and coming undone, adding to her beauty.

He was surprised when she asked for them to talk. It was something that he didn't expect to come from her so soon, but he wouldn't question it. She was wound up so tight that if she wanted to share something about herself, he wasn't going to stop her.

She sat quietly at the kitchen table, staring at her hands, unmoving in her silence. He got up out of the cushioned chair to sit across from her at the table.

"You asked about the scar on my leg," she said, not looking at him.

"I did."

Her hands were clasped together now, her face taut. "It was raining and cold outside. It wasn't quite spring. Boden was just a babe and we were out of food. I nursed him and put him in the bassinet in front of the fire to stay warm.

"I left Ranger to guard Boden as I went out into the oncoming storm to hunt. I found a small boar not far from here. The rain was coming down so hard when I found it. I shot an arrow, but my sighting was off. I clipped him on the shoulder and had to hunt it down."

Locryn's face was angered. He couldn't imagine a woman hunting a boar. The beasts were hard to kill, even small ones. Their skin was tough, and their tusks sharp. They were ornery beasts who did not mind taking on something bigger than them. Even the best of hunters did so in large groups. But this woman claimed to do so all on her own.

"He wasn't hard to track," Jordie continued. "The rain was so heavy that there was nothing but mud everywhere. I followed him down to the riverside another three hundred feet from where I shot him, dead." She looked at him, brows knit together. "I pulled a knife from my boot, to make sure it was dead, but my footing slipped and he caught my leg on his short tusk. It was too wet and muddy to dress it, so I dragged it home. Boden was still thankfully sleeping."

Locryn's brows furrowed.

"At least we had food," she commented.

"What makes ye think ye can take on a boar, lass? Even warriors don't do it alone."

"I was hungry. But you wouldn't know anything of that, would you?"

"So, hunger made ye an eejit?"

"What?"

122

"Stupid!"

She scowled. "What would you have had me do?" she asked. "It's not like you were around to help. No one was!"

Locryn instantly deflated.

She was right.

Jordie turned away from him, arms crossed. Scowling out the window. He knew she couldn't see anything. It was dark and cold. It was just a distraction to keep her from looking at him.

He couldn't imagine walking in her shoes, as a woman, a mother, alone in this small place. Yet, she did so and survived. Somehow, she made it. For seven years, she made it in this harsh world.

Locryn let out a slow, long breath. His eyes roamed her face, admiring her every feature. Even when angry, she was strikingly beautiful. Her hair was swept off to the side, falling down past her voluptuous breasts. Her tanned face glowed against the backlight of the small fire in her hearth.

"I be the middle child," he began. "I have an older brother and a younger sister, Thomas and Marcy."

He had never spoke of his home or family before to anyone. Not even to his friends or his best friend. But she glanced in his direction, so that was a start.

"Me mum be Julia. Thomas took over as laird a few years ago when me da, Conner, passed away. So, me mother still tries to reign, while Laird Thomas be the true ruler o' Drensent. She does ferget that fact sometimes," he said with a smile.

Jordie joined him at the table and placed a hand over his. After that, it seemed easier for him to discuss himself. He went on about his family, his brother's adorable little daughter, and his favorite things to do. She even laughed with him, relaxing a bit and showing her softer side.

Jordie, he found, was actually quite funny. He began to find he loved the way she tucked her stray hairs behind her ears before leaning forward, her head cocked to the side as she asked him questions, her eyebrows raised in wonder and her lips fixed to the side with a smile. He stayed by her side late into the night.

She tried to get up once to restoke the fire, but he pushed her back down into the chair and handled the fire himself. Then he went outside into the darkness to get more firewood and to check on her animals.

"I am so happy you two are hitting it off so well," Aramoren said as he stretched like a sleepy dog in the light of the cottage window. "It's about time."

"Aramoren," Locryn nodded. "Good evenin'."

The shifter yawned, revealing all of his sharp teeth. "I cannot wait to get my house back tomorrow! What time are you leaving?"

"Dawn, or a wee bit after."

"Perfect. Well, good night," Aramoren said and trotted off into the dark forest.

Locryn opened the cottage door and set the wood by the hearth as he fed the fire. He glanced over his shoulder at Jordie who was curled up in the chair watching him. She smiled intermittently but each gentle look was soon replaced by confusion.

"What be wrong, lass?"

Her sweet face softened, as she yawned, covering her mouth with the back of her hand. "I never expected this," she said softly.

"Expected what?"

"To begin to like you."

He didn't know what to say to that. She was hostile earlier, verging on physical aggression. She used her words to try to inflict pain. Jordie was a woman who didn't want to seem weak so she hid behind a blustering façade. But here she was before him, curled up on the small chair like a cat, looking sleepy and almost happy.

Locryn smiled and reached out to hold her hand. "Ye ready ta leave here tomorrow?"

•••••

Jordie's dark brows knitted together.

She hadn't thought about where she would live. She knew she would be leaving with him, but as to where she would stay, whether it be in a castle with him or out with the clan, she didn't know what Locryn wanted to do. Staying with the clan would be preferable, but knowing Locryn, that wouldn't happen.

Mainly, what would her son think? Would he be all right with leaving? Would he be accepted as part of Locryn's clan and family? Would she? Or would everything there be just like how it was here?

It was moving all so fast, and everything was as murky as a swollen stream after a storm. It was out of her control, and once she was married, Locryn would have complete control over them both. She wasn't sure she wanted that or would like it. But she also didn't have much of a choice.

Should she not marry, her father would bring the hammer down upon her head in such a way that it would make their lives even more difficult. If she did marry this man, things would be different. There was no winning here, only a choice between two paths.

But which path to follow?

Jordie decided to be brave and broach the question she wanted to know. "Where will we live?"

"In the castle, lass. Drensent be big enough."

Uncertainty crossed her face like an ocean storm hitting land. Living in the castle with him, his family, his parents—that was something she wasn't sure she could handle. She hadn't lived with anyone save her for son. She wasn't sure she could handle that all at once.

How long does it take to get to Drensent anyway? she thought.

She sat up straighter in the chair, cocking her head to the side. She fell silent at that. "Would I even be welcome?" she finally asked.

126

If his people knew about her past, then they would be suspicious and she could count on them being unkind. And mayhap if his mother knew about her, then surely, she would be unforgiving and intolerant.

Nay, this so-called match just wouldn't work. It couldn't. He was too good for her. He is too kind, too caring, too righteous, and he wanted to marry her solely because he was the last man standing. Because he was an honorable man who pitied her.

Jordie shuddered.

Could she leave here? What would she take? What would he allow her to take with her, if anything? Would he still be tolerant and understanding when they arrived on his land, his terms, his rules?

She looked at the stain on the floor by the beam. Jordie, walked over to it, bending down to touch the spot one last time. Locryn would demand her to leave. To go live with him, to share a bed with him in a castle. Her body trembled. Fear and sweat trickled down her spine. Jordie swallowed. She had to do this for her son. In the end, this was all for him.

Jordie rose to her feet and without looking at him said, "This is where I had Boden. I had just come in from killing a broeshilak, dressing it, salting the meat to hang over a fire to smoke cure. Thunder and rain were pouring down when I finally finished."

He waited.

"I was scared. But I fought through that fear and here we are today, seven years later. With the help of Aramoren, of course. I have done my best for my son and I know he needs a father," she paused and looked at him. "What promise can you give me, to let me know you won't leave us, that you won't change your mind and desert us?"

"Lass, I wilna leave ye." Locryn walked up to her and took her hand, gazing into her amber eyes that now looked at him with so much sorrow and uncertainty. "I do so swear ta ye, Jordie."

CHAPTER FOURTEEN

He could see that she still had trouble believing him. Even if she didn't say a word, it was written all over her face. Suddenly she left the room.

"Lass?" he questioned.

Curious, Locryn followed her.

He watched her as she lifted the small chest onto her bed. The quilt that was on top, was folded down and ready to be packed. She had emptied her chest on her bed where only three garments laid, two pairs of pants and a tunic. She had no stockings. She had no little slippers that women wore in his castle. The woman had next to nothing, yet she was taking it.

He watched her fold and pack the meager possessions. He watched her stuff three long candles into the trunk. Then she moved past him to the kitchen. Was she planning on bringing everything with her? Didn't she know he would give her everything she would need?

"Lass, what do ye think yer doin'?" he asked, growing steadily irritated.

"Being prepared."

"Prepared fer what?"

"In case you change your mind," she said. "In case, as you so promised, you let us go if—or when—it doesn't work out between us."

Locryn crossed his arms. "And where d'ye think ye would go, lass?"

"Wherever I please."

It bothered him that she didn't take him at his word. That she thought he was incapable of providing for her. That she didn't trust in him to do right by her. Instead, she continued to pack. Once everything fit into her chest, she set it down on the floor and walked over to the old cushioned chair that was before the fire and sat.

Jordie was in a conundrum. One part of her was willing to let go of her control and pass the burden of providing onto his shoulders. But another side of her wanted to be prepared for anything to happen, like she was counting on him to desert her.

She let out a long sigh. It was a sigh of defeat, like she accepted what was going to happen and took it with resolve. It was a sigh of a damaged woman acknowledging her broken pieces.

Jordie stared blankly into the fire. Merle poked his head over the ladder. Jordie got him down, putting him in her lap, snuggling him like a fearful child does a doll.

"They don't miss me, do they?" she asked Locryn, his eyes never leaving hers. "My sisters. They don't miss me."

A lone tear tracked its way down her cheek. It took all her control not to give way to her emotions.

Locryn couldn't tell her that they didn't know her. He couldn't tell her that the one sister he interacted with didn't care enough to ask about her. He yearned to hold this woman, to take her in his arms and never let her feel lonely again.

But he couldn't. He looked at her, shifting his feet. He had no idea what to say.

"Lass," he finally said, "ye should get some rest."

He watched her rise out of her chair, sniffling. She wiped her eyes with the back of her hand. She brushed past him, not even acknowledging him as she went inside her chamber.

She sat on the edge of her bed, removing her boots. The pain on her face was something he cared not to see again. She missed her sisters, her family—the same people who left her to her own devices were the same people she loved.

She laid her head on the bed, closing her eyes.

She was tired. Her anxiety finally took its toll. Locryn walked into the bedroom, putting a blanket on her sleeping body. She was curled up in a ball, with her right arm crooked to cradle her head, her left hand came to rest on her other arm. Her small body was on the other side of the bed, her back against the wall and her knife in between her knees.

He walked back out of the chamber, going to the chair by the hearth. They would all leave with him in the morning.

From here on out, they would eat whatever and whenever they wanted.

He would get Boden new boots and clothes. He would get Jordie a dress with soft warm slippers for her feet instead of the tough leather boots that went halfway up her calves. Without a doubt, there would be a battle ahead of him with her. She wouldn't want to take anything from him at all for she would feel like she owed him back.

Locryn started to fall asleep in the chair. He could hear the stillness of the house, of everyone peacefully breathing. It appealed to him.

He drifted off in the chair easily.

He woke with a start when he heard scuffling footsteps. Boden made his way down the loft ladder and tiptoed into the bedroom. He poked his small head inside, but Locryn called him back so he wouldn't wake his mother.

"What woke ye, Boden?" Locryn asked the lad.

"I want to know something, my lord," he said. "You won't hurt my mum, will you?"

"Nay, I wilna hurt her."

Boden nodded, his little face scrunched in thought. "So, what does this mean for us? Are we going to live with you?"

"Aye, in a castle," Locryn said, pulling Boden on his knee. "Ye will have yer own room, yer own bed. I will get ye a horse ye can ride."

Boden smiled wide.

"All men need ta learn it, ye ken. Ye will get some smarts put in that wee head o' yers too."

132

Boden smiled but then looked sad. "So," he paused, "will this mean yer my da?"

Locryn nodded. "Aye, when I marry yer mum, she will be me wife and ye will be me son."

"You will get her a ring?"

"Aye."

"I'm scared, my lord," Boden admitted.

"It's all right ta be afraid, ye ken. I be afraid when I go inta battle," he told the boy. "Want ta tell me what ye be afraid o'?"

Boden sighed. "I am not afraid for me. I am afraid for Mum."

"How so?"

Boden looked sadly into Locryn's eyes. "No one here likes her that much. They call her mean things behind her back. And I don't understand it because she isn't mean at all. I just want Mum to be happy where people don't say mean things."

Locryn didn't know what to say.

His heart never felt so heavy for one woman. Her perceptive son knew how truly alone she was. Her son wanted her to be happy, to be accepted by a clan. Boden wanted so much more for her than what she wanted for herself.

"I swear ta ye, lad, it will be different with me."

Boden nodded, wrapping his small arms around his bulky body.

Locryn mussed his head. "Get ta bed, Boden. We will leave in the morn and we will stop fer some sweet sugar buns along the way."

"What are those?" Boden asked, eyes wide.

Locryn sighed. He was going to buy a dozen sugary buns so Boden could eat them all.

"Well, that just means ye be in fer a treat."

•••••

She could hear them talk. She knew when her son was out of bed. It was that innate maternal instinct. What she didn't expect was for Locryn to talk to her son. She also didn't expect her son to ask Locryn all those questions.

It broke her heart, hearing his small voice asking the big man if he would hurt her. Then her son asking if Locryn was to be his father. Without even a hint of hesitation, Locryn said that Boden was his son.

His son!

But what really shattered her was when Boden told the lord that her clan's people were mean and that no one liked her. It wasn't a lie. But she didn't expect her son to be so observant. And all her son wanted was for life to be different for her. And then those damned tears welled up for what seemed like the hundredth time that day.

She tried her best to not let them hear her cry. It was so hard not to sniffle. It was hard to not let them hear her blubber like a wailing babe. But the tears continued to stream down her face.

Finally, she lay still, gathering herself back together. They would be leaving in the morning. He said as much. That didn't give her time to make arrangements for her animals or her household items, but knowing this man, even briefly, she suspected he had thought of that.

"Can I take my animals with us?" she heard her little boy ask.

"Aye, lad, ye can."

"Good. We have two kittens and a cow, a goat, and a few hens," Boden said. "Mum got me a goat for my birthday. She sold her fancy ring to do it. She does a lot for me. I am glad we can take the animals with us. I will take care of them. I do so swear it, I will."

"Boden, lad, the kitten and the pup, aye, but the other animals, nay. Once yer mum and I be married, well, that makes ye the laird's son and ye wilna be takin' care o' beasties anymore."

"What does that mean?"

"It means ye will have bigger responsibilities as a man. It means ye might, if somethin' happens ta me brother who be laird, follow in me footsteps and be a laird yerself one day."

"I will be a laird?" She could picture Boden's amazement. "What if I don't want to be?"

"We will cross that bridge if we get there, but fer now, ye need ta sleep, and I have ta go settle a few things, all right?"

"Where are you going?"

"I have ta see if I can get a ring fer yer mum and a wagon fer the beasts ta ride in."

"All right! I'll go lay down but I might be too excited to sleep."

"Be a good lad and protect yer mum while I be gone."

The ladder creaked as her son climbed back into his loft.

"I'm getting a dad soon," she heard him whisper.

●●●●●

Locryn smiled at the excited boy. He had arrangements to make. Whatever hour it happened to be, Robert was going to pay him what Jordie was rightfully owed. She deserved it after all the years of being ignored by her own family.

Locryn took a long look around the place his bride called home. It was going to be so hard on her to leave this place. It was comfortable and cozy, but she needed a fresh start in life.

Hand on the latch, he left for the castle. The night had slipped away faster than he realized, and there was still so much that needed to be done.

136

CHAPTER FIFTEEN

Winter reached out its clawing hand, freezing everything it touched, including Locryn's breath. He stuffed his hands deep into his pockets. As he walked back to the castle keep, he couldn't help but think on this woman and her son. His soon-to-be wife and his new son. She was so guarded, so suspicious, with the wheels in her mind turning all the time, debating whether to fight or to fly away. She was bold, always ready to prove her worth when she didn't have to prove anything at all.

By Corwaithe, it be bloody freezin', he thought.

His wife would need to be bundled up, but from what he saw of her things last night, she didn't have anything that would keep her warm enough for the journey. What she really needed was a nice, thick fur coat, but he wasn't going to buy one for her from these same people who shunned her. Nay, he would buy her one from a town along the way.

Dawn broke over the whispering wood. It was quiet, something he would have to learn to appreciate but would rarely have with Boden. The lad certainly loved to talk.

Locryn entered the keep through the dining hall door. Serving women were already busy readying tables and plates for the morning meal. He walked past them, going up the spiral staircase to the second door on the left.

His bag was still in the chair where he left it. His cloak lay on the bed, next to his sword. And something else was there. A note and a fawn leather sack. Locryn walked over to the bed, picking up the parchment.

Here is money to take her back with you. It is enough to pay the priest and to get some gruel, for her at least, and a stable for her and her son. She belongs to you now. Thanks for taking the burden of the bitch off my shoulders.

Happy Marriage.

Robert Duvoir

He was livid from the malicious note, but even more so by the coins. Three silver coins and a handful of coppers lay in that small leather sack. One silver was enough for one night in an inn, with meals and baths included. However, it was not even enough for clothes and boots, which they desperately needed. Hell, it took ten coppers to buy a plain tunic, so a dress had to be more.

He had in his own bag twenty coppers and four silvers. Each silver was twenty coppers, so they had one hundred and sixty coppers to get them from Veiled Hills to Drensent in winter. One night in an inn, which included a bath for each of them, stabling for the animals, and all of their hot meals, was a silver.

Locryn was not happy.

He knew the journey took at least five days but with the weather, he didn't know if it would take longer. Snow fell hard on this side of the Lost Warrior River. A three-day journey could easily turn into a week.

Locryn gathered his things and stormed out of the room. Storming back in, he grabbed the quilt off the bed. Jordie deserved new bedding. But he wasn't done. He decided she needed the sheets as well, along with the pillows and anything else of damned use.

He looked around. On the table by the wash basin were glass jars with stoppers of fragrance. He took them. He turned slowly in a circle, looking for anything else, but found not much.

He made his way down the staircase, arms overflowing with jumbled linen, and found the priest sitting at a table, already drinking heavily.

With a deep scowl, he approached the man. He set the mass of cloth down, wadding it to be carried under his arm along with the glass bottles tucked inside.

"Ye were supposed ta be here last night," Locryn said.

The priest smacked his lips. "Doesn't matter any longer."

Locryn cocked an irritated brow. "What d'ye mean?"

The priest smiled. "Surely you have heard of the Kedavirsta Emoratta."

If that pile of horse dung did this, Locryn thought, *he would have done the worst thing a father could do to a daughter.*

The Kedavirsta Emoratta was a piece of paper that stated that a person was so lowly that not even the divine Goddess Corwaithe could ever recognize the human being as a part of her world. A ruling leader wrote up the decree and a priest had to sanction the paper commemorating it into fruition. And once it was so, the Goddess would eradicate that person from her world, so that not even their soul would have a place in eternity. That person would be forever gone.

If Robert Duvoir did this to his daughter, then Locryn would have to fight to get her recognized by his people, for this type of punishment was saved for the vilest of human beings. And Jordie wasn't one—or so he believed.

"D'ye plan on doin' that ta someone?"

"I plan on giving this paper my seal should Jordie not marry you."

The blanket dropped out of Locryn's arms as he picked the priest up by his robes and dragged the man over the table. "She be marryin' me now, priest, so give me that damned paper!"

The priest clutched the parchment with a smug smile. "Shall we?"

It took everything in him not to beat the man. Priest or not, no one deserved this kind of horrific treatment. It made him wonder what else she had done. If her bedding a man was it, then this was wrong. But he needed to know if that was truly it. Surely, there had to be more to it than she was truthfully letting on.

With profound anger at the situation, Locryn picked up the quilt with one hand while the other dragged the priest behind him. They were going to the house he was about to take Jordie from. If he was at all.

• • • • •

Morning came and went and still no Locryn. She got the eggs collected, the cow and goat milked, and herself fed, but no Locryn. In short, she was livid. He said they were leaving in the morning and yet it wasn't morning any longer. He wasn't even here!

Aramoren waited impatiently in the kitchen, rocking back and forth in his chair. Jordie tried to ignore the annoying shifter but his repeated sighs drove her crazy. Where was Locryn?

He had left. Just like she knew he would. No one would ever stick around long enough to want them both, to love them both as their own. It was all a grand lie.

She sighed. *I should have known better.*

Thankfully, Boden was still sleeping up in the loft. She would have to break the news to him that they were not leaving after all. She could just picture the disappointment on his small handsome face.

141

In truth, she hated Locryn for filling her son's head with false promises. She hated him and his kindness from last night. She hated most of all that she allowed him into her life and this is what she got in return.

Jordie went back inside after splitting some wood, slamming the door behind her. She began unpacking her chest. Aramoren growled behind her, shifting back into his dog form. She turned around to see her father's slime ball of a priest riding toward the house. Locryn drove a team of horses pulling a wagon.

Why is there a quilt next to Locryn? she wondered. *Why does he have all that linen too?*

Locryn yelled something at the priest and then came storming inside her home, slamming the door and coming within inches of her face. He was impressive when he was angry. His muscles bulged, the veins in his face and neck popped, his arms were thick and tense. The scar across his chest glowed bright red.

"Tell me now," he seethed, "why yer da and the priest would do this?" He shoved a sheet of parchment into her chest.

She took the paper and her hands went cold. Her face went pale. This was worse than any death sentence. Her father ordered her to be executed and eradicated by the Goddess. Numbly, she looked at Locryn who glared back at her with accusing eyes.

Instantly, she knew that he thought of her as something so vile. There would be no wedding, no marriage, no happily-ever-after, even if that did somehow exist. There would be nothing for her now.

142

"All I have ever done was love a man, and this," she said, holding up the paper, "is what I receive in return for that blind, stupid love. I have suffered childbearing, child-rearing, hunger, cold, pain, sadness—endured and overcame it all by myself." She looked to the loft, where the sleeping Boden lay. "All I ask, whatever is to become of us, or me, please take my son with you. Let him have a chance at a better life with you."

Jordie turned back around and began unpacking her things. In a daze, she set the forks and spoons back on the counter. She took out the quilt and laid it on the back of the cushioned chair. There would be nothing for her now.

The priest was outside, waiting to sign the paper, and then she would be erased from this world. All she could think about was her son. How would he live without her—if Locryn would even take her son with him. Was there enough time to handle all of her affairs?

She stole at glance at the man who was once her future husband. He stood in the center of her small home, looking at her pitifully as she shuffled around in her daze.

"What?" she dared to ask.

Locryn sighed. "Jordie, pack yer things, lass. Yer still ta be me wife."

Shocked, she rounded on him, yelling her frustrations at him, "You're an asshole!"

"Well, what d'ye expect?" he roared back. "Yer father ordered this!"

How dare Locryn! she growled to herself.

Jordie crumpled to the floor with anger and relief. She was angry with her father for being so abnormally cruel, and angry with Locryn for thinking the absolute worst of her. But she was also relieved that she wouldn't be dying. She didn't want to have to sit and explain to her son what was to happen.

Damn that man, she cursed, tears rolling down her cheeks.

He was always questioning her, doubting her. And if she refused to marry him, then she was going to die. Like her father promised, he would find a way to break her. This never-ending cycle of having to belong to someone or something and no one ever leaving her be, leaving her in peace. It was always something.

She strode over the door, opening it into the cold cloudy morning. "Priest, get your dumbass over here and marry us before I cut out your liar's tongue."

She was so angry.

Angry that the man she was marrying doubted her. Angry that her father ordered her to be eradicated. She wanted to run off and just scream, maybe cry a little more—to be alone enough to pull herself together.

But now was not that time.

The priest waddled into her home, stinking of ale and clutching another piece of paper. He laid it on the table. Jordie read it, making sure it was the paper they needed to sign to be married to each other and not some other lying piece of garbage.

Aramoren let out a low growl.

Jordie scowled at the smug man. "Marry us and make it quick. I've got things to do."

The priest smiled. "Another round of fornication, I imagine?"

Jordie punched him in the nose. "Now," she began, shaking her hand out, "make it short and to the damn point. And you," she turned to Locryn, "I might be married to you, but I can already tell you despise me, and I will tell you right here and now that the feeling is mutual. However, being married to you is better than being dead."

Her head hurt.

The emotions warred inside of her, begging to be released in some way.

But mainly, her heart hurt.

It felt like it might fall out of her chest and onto the floor while she bled out. It bothered her that these were her choices in life—infinite death or married into a living abyss. How did it ever come to this? And was there even a way out of it?

She didn't look at Locryn. She didn't look at the priest. She focused her gaze on the floorboards under her feet. When it came her turn to speak, she did so dutifully, without feeling, completely detached from it all.

Soon it was all over. She signed her life away to a man who considered her to be the pile of manure he had gotten roped into marrying. When in turn, it was she who married the most unfeeling asshole in all of Castre. Jordie signed her name to the paper and walked outside. She stood in the cold, trying to let it fill her.

Locryn stood in the doorway, watching her.

"I will be right back," she yelled, taking off at a dead run.

She had to go find a place to be quiet. To let her soul settle. She was married now. Married to a man who thought so little of her and here she was, already running away. She didn't even kiss him. And sure, as she was breathing life, she didn't want to either.

Jordie ran until her lungs burned in the cold air. She ran until her sides hurt and her heels were sore. She ran until she was far enough away from it all to feel something deep and what she felt broke her.

Her foot tripped on a mossy log and she fell to her knees. She turned around, leaning her back against it and cried.

She cried about her mother, her father, the family she lost. She cried about Boden, Lane, Locryn, and how her life had taken so many surprising turns in two days. She sat and cried. She screamed. She beat her fists against the rotting moss-covered log and yelled until her voice became hoarse.

Then she cried because she finally felt better. It was the most freeing type of crying. She was laughing at herself for her stupidity. Laughing at her naïve, trusting nature that something could be right this time around for her family, that something could go right for her.

She laughed.

146

She cried.

"I am so stupid!" she said aloud. "I am so incredibly stupid!"

"Yer no' stupid, lass," Locryn said coming up behind her.

Jordie dried her eyes on the sleeve of her tunic. "Yeah, I must be a special kind of stupid for marrying the likes of you."

"Really?" he said, grabbing her by the arm. "No one just orders the Emoratta on someone withoot somethin' happenin', lass."

"And I told you," she fought him to let her go, "that I have only done that one thing, so you can either accept that or leave! I don't care, but you need to pick!"

Locryn scowled at her but remained silent.

"Pick, you bastard!"

JORDIE IN CHARGE

CHAPTER SIXTEEN

He stood before her, fists on his hips, being challenged by a slip of a woman. She straightened her back, rising up to her full height. She was tall for a woman. Her cherry red hair billowed behind her as the wind picked up around them. Her amber eyes, flecked with golden sparks, dared him, defied him. She glared up at him, her fierce beauty more ethereal than the forest around her.

Jordie was breathing heavily. Her tear-streaked cheeks looked cold and flushed red from crying.

"Fucking pick," she growled, breaking the silence.

He held back a grin.

This woman was wound up so tight. She wanted him to leave her alone. She wanted him to go away and leave her in her ordinary world, but Jordie was his wife now. Things were going to change whether she liked it or not.

"Yer me wife. Yer comin' with me. Yer son be me son. He be comin' with me. So, let's go," he said and started walking back along the path.

Jordie stomped her foot.

"Let's go, lass," Locryn called back.

149

"It's Jordie!" she yelled at him, storming through the brush and pushing past him.

"Yer me wife. I will call ye what I please," he shot back, not at all in the mood to deal with her.

"Fine. You're *my* husband so I will call you exactly what I please."

"It does no' work that way."

She tossed a look over her shoulder. "Aye, it does, dummy. You want to leave here, so let's go. You happen to be wasting daylight."

Locryn felt his resolve slipping a little further.

He reached out and grabbed her by the upper arm, spinning her around to face him. He was furious. She was hiding something from him, that was clear. He planned on doing right by her for a day or so, to see if she would tell him the truth. He was also just done with her cynicism and downright stubbornness.

"Let's get some things cleared up, all right?" he said, his face a mere inch from hers. "Ye will do what ye be told. Ye will live where I tell ye, eat what and when I tell ye, and wear what I tell ye. Yer no' alone anymore and ye wilna act like ye be!"

Fresh tears began to shine in her eyes. "Fine," she replied.

He made Jordie walk in front of him all the way back to her home. A wagon was out in front loaded with her chest and her son's kittens and dog. Thankfully, obedient Boden was in the back of the wagon, still drowsy, resting on his quilts and blankets. Everything she had ever owned fit into the back of this small wagon and he knew she wouldn't leave without it.

Jordie climbed into the back of the wagon to sit with her son. He knew she wanted to be nowhere near him but that was also going to change. He motioned for her to sit up front beside him. Shooting him a disgusted glare, she went to sit on the hard wooden seat beside him.

He knew he was going to have his hands full with her. "Ye can at least look like yer happy ta be leavin', lass."

She turned slowly to face him. "My name is Jordie, all right, dummy? And I am not happy. But being married to you is preferable to being dead and leaving my son motherless. This is all you are ever going to get from me. I do not care whom you bed; we are married in name only." And with that, she straightened up and looked on ahead.

Locryn grabbed her chin, pulling her close to him. "So ye have said, but ye will still do as I say, *lass*."

"We shall see, *dummy*."

"Dinna call me that!" he roared in her face.

"The correct word is 'don't,' so *don't* call me lass."

Locryn growled, letting go of her face, "Had I known ye'd be so verra much trouble, I would no' have ever married ye."

"You brought this upon yourself, you persistent ass. You think I am a pile of garbage because my father brought the Emoratta upon me. This is all because I loved someone," she cast a sidelong glare at him, "and I was willing to trust you!"

Locryn didn't know what to say.

"It's about time," Aramoren said, coming beside the wagon in his dog form. "Safe journey. Oh, and Jordie, you're going to think about coming back here. I suggest you don't. You will never stumble upon my home again. Trust this man."

Aramoren loped off to his cottage door. "And, Locryn," the animal called out, "Jordie doesn't tell lies. Believe her." Aramoren opened the door and went inside.

Locryn shook his head. *Those creatures be somethin' else.*

He slapped the reins to get the horses moving. They rode through the woods and the vegetation closed on the path behind them. True to the shifter's word, Jordie never set eyes on that cottage again. And she never looked back. She never cried for what she lost.

No one waved her off, not even the guards at the gates of the castle when they rode by. Everyone stood still as stone, watching the horses clatter the wagon along. They passed the end of the village and they were out of Veiled Hills for good.

Relief seemed to register on her face. He snapped the reins, urging the horses to trot. Jordie shifted in her seat and the glower faded from her face as she took in the passing scenery. But if she caught him looking at her, her scowl would return.

152

Towards mid-morning, Boden woke with a flurry of questions, peppering them both. Jordie chatted with her son but said nothing to Locryn. Boden played with his puppy and his kittens. For the most part, he was a good lad.

They stopped a few times to relieve themselves behind a tree or a bush. Locryn put Boden on top of his horse, where he rode bareback beside the wagon for a while. The boy was a naturally good rider and the horse liked him immensely.

Noon came and went.

Locryn found out a good deal about both of his new family members. Boden was a wellspring of information, especially since his new wife still wouldn't speak to him. It bothered him, for it seemed to prove her guilt over something.

Sunset came with a flurry of color in the clear skies. It was going to be chilly night but a night without snow.

Locryn parked the wagon in an outcropping of trees and unhitched the team of horses. He hammered two stakes in the ground and tied the horses to it for the night. His wife watched him, arms folded.

He called Boden over and the two went into the forest to gather wood. Jordie tried to follow but he told her to sit and stay. He never meant to treat her like a dog. But he was still so furious with her for lying. There had to be something more to her than just having a son.

He came back with wood, setting it down near her. She hurriedly wiped the tears off her face, acting as if she was never crying to begin with. He tried to ask her if she was all right, but she wouldn't speak. She ignored every question

153

he asked. He never thought a woman not speaking to him would bother him, but it did.

He also never thought it would bother him so when she told him that she despised him. Many women were mad over him. Regina was mad that he never liked her in the way she liked him, but she wasn't the most attractive person during the day. At night and with enough ale, she looked a lot better. She was always so willing, but waking up next to her in the morning required more ale.

Hazel was a gorgeous woman, but she bedded anyone that had a cock and two feet. He took her up to his tower chamber often. Getting her to bed him was like asking a dog if it wanted a bone. However, Hazel was much more pleasing to wake up to, inspiring more rounds of naked fun.

Locryn looked at his wife. She was the only person he could bed now since they had taken their vows of marriage. He wondered what her skin would feel like against his, and how warm her voluptuous body would be to his touch. He wanted to slant his lips over hers, but he couldn't bring himself to do it.

He heard her stomach rumbled with hunger.

"Be ye hungry, lass?"

Jordie stared at him as if she could see through him. "No," she said flatly.

Locryn snickered.

"Boden, lad, get more wood fer the fire, will ye?" Locryn asked her son.

When the boy was gone, Locryn went over to where she was sitting. He sat down next to her, his legs over hers so she couldn't get away. Before she could do anything with her hands, he grabbed them too.

"Yer goin' ta talk ta me," he said, "I have had enough o' yer attitude today."

"I don't want to speak to you," she said. "If I did, I would."

"Why be ye this way?"

"What way?" she asked. "Angry?"

"Aye, why ye be this way? Yer oot o' Veiled Hills and yer still no' happy."

"I wonder why," she shot back.

"Aye, me too," he said. "Why dinna ye like me?"

"It is you who dislikes me," she countered. "I see it on your face. The mistrust, the revulsion. I did nothing but love a man. Why can't you trust me that having Boden was all I did?"

"Yer father put an Emoratta on yer head!"

Jordie hung her head, crying into her outstretched arms he held.

When he first got a good look at her, he thought her the most beautiful woman he had ever laid eyes on. And after getting to know her, he found a woman who was so guarded that her heart had become like a stone towards other people. He found a woman who was going to be hard to love.

He found a woman who was fearful of trusting someone again.

Locryn pulled her into his arms. She stiffened at first, but as she sobbed against him, he hesitantly caressed her back and she relaxed into his embrace.

"I be sorry," he whispered.

Jordie sniffled. "I was willing to put aside my hurt and trust again," she mumbled into his shoulder. "I'm so stupid."

Boden walked up and Jordie leaned off of Locryn. The boy set down a large bundle of wood, all too proud to show that he carried it on his own. Locryn tried to make her smile as he told the tale of how he pilfered the quilt, linens, and perfumes out of his room. Boden seemed to think it was funny but still felt the need to admonish Locryn that stealing things wasn't nice. Jordie only cracked a slight smile but said nothing.

Locryn decided to go hunting for a little bit to think on all that she had said. He didn't wander far from their camp, just enough to get into the woods to look for something to eat. He looked behind him to see Boden following him, so he called to the lad and together they hunted.

It was dark when they both came back to camp, each with two rabbits in hand. Boden sat down next to his mother and began skinning the animal. For being seven, he was adept at survival, like his mother.

The moonlight glimmered down on her dark head, casting shadows of light upon her face. It was beautiful the way Jordie's gorgeous face burned brightly against the night. If it wasn't for the sour expression when she looked at him, she would have been even more beautiful.

"He did good, wife," Locryn commented about Boden's hunting.

Jordie smiled and mussed her son's hair, kissing him on the head. "He is a good boy."

"Thanks, my lord," Boden said.

"Lad, I be married ta yer mum now," he said. "Ye can call me Da."

"I can?"

Locryn nodded, "Aye, ye can."

Boden smiled a mile wide.

Her scowl was removed from her beautiful face, replaced with a look of vulnerability—one that she was too proud to recognize. She picked up Boden's rabbits and skinned them herself. Boden came over to him, chatting about their hunt.

Locryn roasted the rabbit and taught Boden how to season it with the things around them. The lad was like moss, soaking up every last bit of knowledge Locryn fed him.

Jordie watched on in silence. She had loving looks in her amber eyes only for Boden. She had a beaming smile only for Boden. Everything about her was solely for the boy.

And he knew why.

He knew he hurt her. It wasn't his words that did it. It was the way he looked at her as he said them and every moment after. He realized now that Aramoren was right. She hadn't lied to him when she said she was innocent of the Emorata's curse. The question was, how could he win this amazing woman back? For her silence would be the death of him.

Locryn got up off the ground, going back to the wagon for the blankets. He placed one over his wife's shoulders and sat beside her. Boden was busy turning the rabbit on a spit. Locryn glanced over at his wife, who was looking at her son with a faint smile.

"I be sorry," he said.

Doubt flickered across Jordie's face. Slowly, she turned back to watch her son.

Locryn sighed.

He was going to have to find a way to win her heart.

CHAPTER SEVENTEEN

Four more days of traveling and they arrived at Drensent Castle, just as the dawn waked the sky with fire. Locryn told them yesterday that he wanted to get home as soon as he could, so they traveled into the night by the light of the full moon. The sky was cloudless and the roads clear of snow, so not wanting to chance a storm, they pressed on.

Now they were here.

She had never seen a horizon so wondrous in all her life. Even at home, with the breaking of dawn glowing brightly, it seemed dull compared to this. The heavens appeared as if they were set ablaze. The fire in the sky woke up the trees, setting them scorching with brilliant light.

Jordie caught her breath at the sight.

Even the trees were different. Where she lived, they were smaller—maples, dogwoods, birches, and wonderful weeping willows, all whispering of faeries and secrets. Here, there was a wildness, a deep-seated hunger of pines and firs wanting to reach the heavens. To touch the inferno that burned across the sky.

She watched the road intently, wondering what was beyond the last rising hill, wondering what she would find next. Jordie leaned forward in her seat as the wagon and horses climbed the hill.

Again, Jordie caught her breath.

It was the most magnificent castle she had ever seen. The massive edifice loomed over a cliff in the mountains. It had four twisting peaks, spires that rose wide and tall with arrow slits in their sides. An enormous wall surrounded it. This was a castle that could withstand any siege.

They were still some ways off but already she was nervous. Her hands felt clammy as she gripped the sides of the wagon. For the first time, she realized how truly powerful her husband and his family must be.

A thick black iron portcullis blocked them from entering. And it also blocked her from leaving. How would she escape should Locryn keep proving that he was an asshole? She would be trapped behind these iron bars.

The whole way here, Locryn tried to be kinder. She had seen it. He tried to soften his words and start conversations, but she could still read the slight look of mistrust and resentment on his face.

Jordie glanced sideways at her husband. Focused on the gate that they plodded towards, he whistled, announcing their approach. Her hands gripped the wagon tighter. For the first time in a long while, she was unbelievably nervous.

Locryn continued to stare straight ahead, fixated on their destination.

Jordie started to quake but not from the cold. Her eyes darted back at the iron gate. People would soon be

160

approaching. And since Locryn whistled, they would be coming quicker now.

And here they came.

Boden gazed around in wonder. Her young son peppered Locryn with questions. The burly man answered every one, and Boden hung on every word he said. Her new husband seemed to enjoy going into detail about their new home.

Jordie hung her head.

It would be selfish of her to leave Locryn since her son loved the man already. Even Merle seemed smitten with him. In a sense, she felt emotionally betrayed. Everyone liked this man and trusted him. Everyone but her. She couldn't bring herself to have any feelings for this man yet.

Was she the only person to see him for what he truly was? Was she the only person still sane enough to figure out this man despised her? Or was she seeing what she wanted to see to make it easier on her to dislike him enough to leave?

Jordie sat in the wagon, her back straight as a rod, riding through that black gate of doom like the princess she was. She gazed above everyone who stopped to stare at her as they rode through. Only her son was oblivious to their attention.

Jordie hadn't spoken much to Locryn in days and she liked it that way. But now, passing all of these people and all of these homes, she wanted one of her own. She wanted her house back. Locryn stopped the wagon in the middle of center square and stood on the bench seat overlooking his people.

Dear Corwaithe, he is going to make a bloody announcement, she inwardly groaned. *That son of a bitch!*

She desperately wanted to disappear with a snap of her fingers like Aramoren. She wanted to die a thousand deaths in an oven and then be buried under pig droppings—anything other than face these people now.

Locryn stood.

Jordie felt her hands shake, so she sat on them.

"Me fellow clansmen, clanswomen, bonny wee lassies, and strappin' young laddies, this be me wife, the Princess Jordie Maria Duvoir o' Veiled Hills, now Princess Jordie Mercendi o' Drensent."

Jordie stood on shaking legs, giving a weak smile and curtsy to her new clan. They in return raised eyebrows of suspicion. Women whispered to their husbands and neighbors. They knew of her already.

Wonderful, she thought, *just like home. Nothing will ever change.*

"And this me new son, Boden," he told them all. "Please make them both feel verra welcome."

With that, he got down off the wagon.

She didn't wait for him to help her down. She jumped off, standing a few feet away from some of the women, feeling foreign in her trews and tunic with a belt around her small waist, a long dagger in her boot, and a hatchet strapped at her side.

162

Then the staring really began.

The women covered their mouths. The men were wide-eyed, averting their glances and shaking their heads. She smiled, wanting to seem polite and genuine to these new people, but they turned away from her. Just like she knew they would.

I am different on the outside, she thought to herself, *but I am not so different on the inside. Stupid people. I wish I could hide away from all of this. Some things won't ever change and now my husband knows it.*

"Ye sure ye married a lass, boy?" one of the men spoke.

And here it starts. She tried to keep her face fixed in a polite smile.

The crowd laughed.

Her face warmed when Locryn made that announcement, but now it really burned. Boden moved beside her, grabbing her calloused hand in his small one and waiting. She looked down at his pale face and gave his hand a reassuring squeeze.

Locryn made a move toward the man who spoke and shook his hand. The man was older with black hair peppered with gray. His belly was rounded and he walked with a limp towards her husband. She saw he was missing two fingers on his left hand and his right eye. But his smile was broad and his eyes were cheery.

"Aye, Grandda, I married a bonny lass," he said, motioning toward her.

163

Mechanically, she dipped her head to the elder man. She made no motion to approach him but stood her ground. It was hard not to run and hide with everyone watching. Her head screamed to take Boden and leave. She didn't want the embarrassment. She didn't want the unacceptance, the hatred, the gossiping, and everything else that came with it.

"Why be the poor lass wearin' men's clothes then?" Locryn's grandda asked.

"Aye, why be she wearin' those horrid clothes?" said an elegant lady. The crowd parted for her as she glided towards Locryn.

Jordie heated.

She could only surmise that this was Locryn's mother, Lady Julia. She wore an emerald dress to match the crown she wore on top of her perfectly coifed hair. Jordie dipped a curtsy and bowed her head, pulling Boden down to drop a knee.

"Rise," the magnificent lady said. "Jordie, be it?"

Jordie nodded.

"So, the shame o' Veiled Hills has made her way here."

Jordie looked down at the ground. She could either let the gossip and shunning of Veiled Hills repeat itself here, or she could stop it all here and now. She could stand up for herself—and for her son.

With narrowed eyes, she turned to the older man. "I wear trews, my Lord Bellamy, because I have been on my own since seventeen. Dresses get in the way and I happen to like trews."

The queen mother stared at her, her mouth open and a hand on her chest. "Shame, indeed."

Jordie pursed her lips.

"Follow me," Julia commanded.

Jordie turned around, grabbing her bow and quiver. She never went anywhere without them. Feeling secure, she let the queen lead her away.

Locryn watched her, but she didn't look back at him. He was still unforgiven and had to prove to her that she meant something different to him. And she knew that he wouldn't, so leaving him wouldn't be an issue for her. Her only concern was for her son who inexplicably adored the man.

Jordie followed Julia across the castle grounds. The long spiraling tower appeared before them in solid rock. Houses close together but were spaced evenly apart and many guards walked along the walls. It was unlike anything she had ever seen. How big was this castle, exactly? It was very impressive.

Julia stopped at the foot of the stairs. "I ken about ye," she said, grabbing Jordie's arm, "I ken what ye done and what yer family says. I be no' an eejit. Keep yer legs closed ta others but open fer me son." With that, Julia let go of her. "Yer room be at the verra top."

Jordie turned to the stairs, then looked down at her son's sad expression.

"And dinna ever disrespect my kin like that in front o' the clan again or *ye* will regret it," the lady said and swept away.

Jordie watched her leave before heading up the stone steps.

It was a slap to the face.

Julia paused at the end of the staircase. "And dinna get me wrong. Me son likes ye, however I dinna. I told him no' ta go, but here we be," she said.

Jordie closed her eyes to block it all away. If she was going to be berated for something, she wished it wasn't in front of her son. He shouldn't have to experience the spite and the revulsion which she seemed to inspire.

Boden squeezed her hand. "What did she mean, Mum?"

"It was an adult remark, my little love. Don't worry over it, all right?"

"Aye, Mum."

They strode up the stairs to the first door. Inside was a small bed and with a chest at the end. A table with a wash basin and a wardrobe stood over in one corner. There was also a small hearth and a window. The room would suit her son just fine. It was better than what he had back home.

Jordie placed a hand on his shoulder and kissed his mahogany head. "Get your animals, love, and settle yourself in your new room."

"All of this is mine?"

"Aye. Go get Merle and your kittens."

166

Boden raced back down the stairs. Jordie shut the door and continued the flight up the stone stairs. Her room was just above her son's and looked much the same.

Jordie unloaded her tools on the bed. She laid the arrows and her bow down, wondering where to store them. Next, she removed her hatchet and knife. Jordie looked around the room and sighed.

This place didn't feel like home. It didn't look like home. It didn't smell like home. To her, it would never be her home. Nothing would. It was clear to her that she wasn't accepted by this clan or her husband's family.

But what choice did she have?

She locked the door so no one would come in and make her more miserable. The queen had offered her a bath, yet she didn't want to bathe like a princess. She wanted to be like everyone else for once in her life. She wanted to mingle, to talk with others about something ridiculous like flowers or how the ground smelled after it rained. But she knew they wouldn't do that here. She would not have a friend.

With a deep breath, she resolved herself to a life of solitude, just like she had done before, but now with a different group of people and in a different place. With the next deep breath, all the anxiety she kept inside burst forward in a torrent of sobs.

●●●●●

His mother came out of the tower with a disgusted look on her face. She waved for him to follow her but he stood there, talking to some of his comrades. There would be plenty of time to catch up with her at the feast tonight, or even after. He already knew what she was going to say about his wife.

Before he left, his mother had opposed his plan to visit Veiled Hills, bidding him to find a wife in Clouneder or Wendren. But he wanted to go to Veiled Hills to see if the rumors about Jordie Duvoir were true. To witness with his own eyes what had become of a powerful king's shameful daughter.

Julia begged him not to go, pleaded with him for hours. She told him that he could choose whomever he wanted to marry as long as he didn't go. His mother made her opinion of his leaving for Veiled Hills very clear to him and also her opinion of Jordie.

But when he went to Veiled Hills, he found something he did not expect. He found a loving and tenacious woman with a heart bleeding for her son. He knew Jordie was more than that, but it was hard to discover what it was when she wouldn't speak.

Locryn sighed, rubbing the back of his neck.

His mother became more challenging to deal with over the years, especially after his father died. She wouldn't stay out of his or his brother's business and disliked Thomas's sweet wife, Ehlowen, for the longest time. But his own wife already had two strikes against her. One, she had a child out of wedlock. And two, he married her against his mother's expressed wishes.

He tried to talk to Jordie during their journey but the woman wouldn't speak a word. Locryn couldn't tell if she simply needed time or if he had hurt her feelings beyond repair. He knew his accusations had hurt her. But it was hard to look at her and not wonder if there could be something else hiding.

Poor lass, he said to himself. *Me mum will probably be nasty ta her and she be already hurt. I need ta somehow make it better.*

He spotted Boden coming out of the West Tower, the boy's new home. A few lads in the clan already came up to him and together they bounded off with a ball. Already Boden was making new friends with the other young boys in the clan. There were several lads his age, so he would grow up with them and make strong friendships.

He watched his son play for a bit before turning back to his own friends.

"She be a tall lass," one man remarked.

The other man nodded. "Aye, Finn, and she wears men's clothing. I think I would have a conniption if I saw my wife in that."

"I agree, Gordon," Finn replied. "I dinnae how ye stand fer it, milaird."

Locryn stood there, taking their views of his wife quietly for a bit. They weren't mean things, just observations of her appearance. Jordie did dress like a man. He hoped to change that in time. He wondered how a beautifully crafted gown would snug her already delicious body and cup her full breasts.

169

"She was poor," Locryn told them, turning back from watching his son. "That be all she had."

Finn looked confused. "A daughter o' a laird poor?"

"Aye, Finn," Locryn said. "She had a son oot o' wedlock, so they left her in a cottage in the woods."

"Corwaithe, Lo," Finn said, "Ye married her oot o' pity? That's sad. Ye can do better. If her own parents didna want her, then that says somethin' right there."

"Aye, Locryn. What Finn says is right," Gordon pitched in.

"There be somethin' about her, lads."

"Aye, something manly," Gordon said.

Finn shook his head. "Ye better dump the lass like a burnt cake."

"And then what?" Locryn asked. "Return her ta the wild with her boy?"

"She be your wife," Gordon shrugged. "Do what you want, but something needs to be done."

"Yer a kinder man than I," Finn said.

"There be somethin' about her, lads," Locryn said again. "I canna put it ta words, but there be somethin' about her that captivates me."

Locryn clapped his friends on the back and headed to the West Tower. He knew that she would put Boden in the first room, so he started climbing straight up to the second room, knowing that she wouldn't want to be near him in the top room they were supposed to share.

It wasn't all his fault. Aye, he did happen to look at her differently since her father ordered the Kedavirsta Emoratta, but so would anyone else. And still he went through with the marriage. There was just something about her that drew him to her. She was honest about her feelings even when she tried to hide them.

Locryn sighed and ran his hand over his face.

They were married now, whether she liked it or not. There was no going back. He paused in front of her door, listening. He heard nothing. Locryn knocked. Then knocked again. Still nothing. So, he went back down the stairs, leaving her be. She would come out when she was ready, even if it was only for her son.

Either way, he would wait for her.

JORDIE IN CHARGE

CHAPTER EIGHTEEN

She snuck out of the West Tower without him noticing. Locryn had his back to her, talking to two other men.

"Ye better dump the lass like a burnt cake," one of them said.

Jordie hung her head but kept walking.

She walked in a straight line wherever she went. Just like at the old home, people got out of her way and stared. Jordie shifted the bow and quiver on her back. If they were going to ignore her, then she would do what she had always done for herself and Boden: provide.

She found her son in the stables before she set out. A few of the boys were watching the horses in the corral. Jordie told him to stay close to the keep and Locryn while she went out. She gave him a big hug and a kiss on the head before heading towards the main gate they came through just an hour before.

Jordie looked at the sun. It wasn't quite mid-morning. Animals would still be out searching for food. It was the perfect time to go hunting.

She stood in the middle of the courtyard looking around at all the people milling about. There weren't as many as she thought there would be, maybe a few hundred. However, there were many more people in the villages she passed along the way, where the ground was fertile.

A line of supply wagons passed under the portcullis. *How wonderful*, she thought. More than likely those arrivals meant there would be a feast tonight to celebrate Locryn's nuptials. Jordie groaned, rolling her golden eyes.

Thank the stars, the heavy portcullis was open, its sharp points hanging over her head as she passed under it. No one hindered her, as she knew no one would. The bright sun slid gracefully through the tree branches, casting a golden shimmering glow on the forest floor. Dust speckles floated around her head like a hovering halo.

Patches of snow lingered where the sun couldn't reach. Leaves from the previous fall clutched each other against the snow, molding underneath, giving off a new and most welcoming aroma to her senses. She loved the smell of the forest.

Jordie walked off the beaten path in search of tracks, looking behind her to see if her husband followed. No one was there.

Thank goodness, she thought. *After what his friends said, I don't care to be followed or spoken to. I cannot believe he just stood there while his friend said to drop me like a burnt cake. But whatever,* she scoffed, *it's not like he ever liked me that much to begin with. He only married me to keep me from being wiped off the face of Castre.*

Jordie let off a sigh of complete, utter relief.

With a smile and a change of heart, she leaned her back against a tall redwood tree and undid the knot on top of her head. Her wild red locks fell in a twisting tumble to the bottom of her back. With deft hands, she braided her hair off to the left side, feeling the coolness of the strands against her cold cheeks.

She made the belt around her waist tighter and checked the knife in her waist belt. With a second glance behind her, she set off in search of prey.

On the way to their new home, they passed so many red holleristo deer. She couldn't believe how many were up this far north. They were bigger than the regular black deer of the valley that she was used to hunting. Red deer had the best meat and were as big as a mule. They were slow, as their legs were not very long, and their antlers made a lot of noise in the woods by constantly hitting on low tree branches.

However, if she did kill a red deer, she would have trouble bringing it back. They were thick creatures with a lot of meat and muscle. They were also very aggressive, which made it dangerous at times. She would have to settle for something smaller like a black deer or a groewindel. Even a broeshilak would be nice, but she doubted they lived this far north.

Broeshilak were her absolute favorite prey. They were small, pig-like creatures with big ears like a rabbit. They had six stumpy legs that moved quickly when frightened, but they stood often quiet and still for a few moments, making them easy to kill. Broeshilak were easy to find for they made snuffling noises when foraging for food.

Back in Veiled Hills, they were abundant. They bred like rabbits and spread out all over her home land, even if they were easy kills. Not many people ate them, although she never figured out why.

Broeshilak or no, anything she brought back would be preferable to nothing. She knew the castle had food. She knew they would have stores. But nothing beat fresh meat. More food would always be welcome.

Her new people would just have to be grateful. Any food was better than being hungry. But she seriously doubted that any of them knew what it was like to starve.

That was one good thing about Locryn. He always made sure that she and Boden ate before he did. He even stopped to buy her son a sweet sugared bun like he promised and a new pair of boots the boy desperately needed to have. Something that she could never give her son, Locryn did. He was a good man and a good new father to Boden. Locryn even got her a coat, which she wore even now.

It was those small considerations that made her appreciate him a little more. He chatted with Boden for hours, answering all of his questions. Locryn opened up a lot on their journey, telling them both about his home and how he was next in line for a throne he didn't want. Instead, he only wanted to have a family.

However, Locryn never did buy her the ring he had promised. That was all right though; she didn't want to wear one anyway. The whole ride here, he never said much to her directly. He would scowl, then soften his face slightly, but then scowl again. She knew that he would never come to love her. It made her heart hurt for what she so desperately wanted to have, but she consoled herself with the hope that maybe someday, someone besides her son and Merle would love her unconditionally.

Locryn is a good man, even if he does scowl, she said to herself. *I just don't understand what else he thinks I could have done. I wish he would believe me and look at me as he did before, with those kind, beautiful blue eyes.*

Jordie sighed.

Twigs broke to her right. Swiftly, she drew her bow and nocked an arrow. A red holleristo deer passed by with her fawn. Jordie ignored the beast, continuing to walk farther, deeper into the woods. There was no way she could down that and bring it back by herself.

She walked around for about an hour before spotting some groewindel.

Silently, she nocked her arrow, aiming for the head of the beast. She wanted to shoot it before it had time to trumpet an alarm. Their screech was a long, wailing, deep-throated echo. With a slow breath out, she released her arrow and got the animal right through its long neck. It fell dead to the ground without the others noticing.

With careful patience, she moved closer to the other groewindels in the trees. Three sat on the branch just above the one she killed. Jordie nocked another arrow, letting it fly through the neck of another beast.

Their wings started to flutter in fright. She knew she had but just a few moments before they all flew off to a different location, leaving the forest silent again. Swiftly, she nocked her third arrow and hit the last one right in the head. And finally, another, again through the neck.

Nature was dependable. It followed a consistent timing. Spring was followed by summer and so on. She knew she could go out hunting and find food.

Jordie stood over her four large birds.

She might not be able to trust Locryn or his people yet. But she could feed them.

She picked up the four large birds, removed the arrows from their willowy necks and the head on the other, and slung the birds across her shoulder. Then she headed back to her new-found dungeon with its high walls, towering rock spires, and impenetrable iron gate.

With a sigh, she trudged back. She kicked up clumps of dirt and moss and sometimes tufts of snow, scattering it to the wind.

I wonder what he is going to yell at me next, she thought. *Or better yet, what will his wonderful mother say. I should have left Veiled Hills years ago. Then this never would have happened. But here I am, married to a handsome yet bothersome man. I just hope that my husband will come around. I'm not that bad of a person. At least, I don't think I am horrible. Am I?*

Unfortunately, she found her way back faster than she would have liked. Guards stood at the entrance on either side, not paying her the slightest bit of attention. To her good fortune, Locryn was nowhere to be seen.

She spotted her son playing in the middle of the castle yard with Merle and a few other lads. Jordie made her way

178

to the main keep, going around to the back where the kitchens most likely would be.

The place was bustling with women and men getting the feast prepared. She rolled her eyes. She wanted nothing to do with this celebration, and if she had it her way, she wouldn't be attending at all.

I will have to wear a damned dress to this, I just know it, she grumbled, *and sit next to all of his wonderful family.*

A portly older woman came up to her after a while. Without a word, Jordie handed the dead creatures over to the woman and walked away.

"Wait!" the woman called out.

Jordie turned around. "Aye, good lady?"

"Did you kill these birds?"

"Aye."

"You have better aim than our regular hunter, Tosh," she praised. "My name id Hester. What is your name?"

"Jordie, it was very nice to meet you. Thank you for that compliment. I hope you are able to put the meat to good use."

Jordie turned to walk away again, but the woman called out to her.

"The same Jordie that is married to Laird Locryn?"

"Aye," she confirmed.

"And he let you hunt?"

Jordie scowled. "We may be married, but he does not control me. He despises me, yet he married me to save me, so my son can have a mother. That is all this is."

She turned to walk away for the third time, but she turned back around.

"I apologize for being short," she said, deflating. "No one has spoken to me in years and I am afraid I am a bit rusty on how to properly converse. Please, let me know if I can be of further assistance to you."

Jordie looked into Hester's eyes before leaving. There was no hatred in them, no disgust, nothing. Her green eyes held kindness and, if she dared to think it, compassion. The first pair of kind eyes she had seen in a long, long time.

I am being stupid again, she thought to herself.

Jordie walked to where she saw her son playing with the other boys and sat down, removing her hunting equipment and setting it in her lap. She smiled at them as they raced around, kicking a ball and yelling. Thankfully, she was out of the way enough to not get struck by a flying ball.

Boden was fitting in, having friends and playing with kids his age. The boys ran with all their might, trying to get a ball past the other team. Her son kicked it away from another small boy and his teammates cheered, yelling 'score' at the top of their lungs.

Jordie laughed.

If her son fit in, if her son had friends, if her son was thriving here in this short amount of time, then she would suck it up and be braver for him. He deserved it.

They continued to play until a loud booming bell rang out, announcing the nooning meal. Boden ran over to her. "Mum," he said excitedly, "my friend Jordan's grandmum invited me over for the nooning meal. May I go please?"

Jordie smiled, hugging him. "Aye, you can go. Tell your friend's grandmother thank you for me."

"She invited you too."

"Oh," she said, surprised. "Would you like me to go?"

Boden nodded vigorously.

Jordie got up off the ground, dusting herself off the best she could. She knew she had to go, not only for her son but to make a good impression on Locryn's clan. It would be expected of her. She swung her gear upon her back as she followed her son, who was busy talking with his new friend, Jordan.

When they reached the cottage, Jordie stopped dead in her tracks. Hester stood before her, smiling and waving her inside.

Jordie smiled politely as she walked towards the woman. The boys ran inside while Jordie stood before the cook, her cheeks turning pink.

"Thank you for inviting my son and I to join you for the nooning meal," Jordie said.

Hester smiled and took her arm in hers. "It is my pleasure to get to know the laird's wife."

"That is quite a title."

Hester laughed. "He doesn't like to be called prince or heir. Most of us call him Lo."

Jordie nodded.

"While I serve lunch to the boys, tell me a little about yourself. We can talk over here," she said, pointing to a table and two chairs that sat at the back of her home.

"We got it, Grandmum," Jordan called. "Come on, Bo, let's eat then play some more! I know a perfect place to catch frogs."

"Bye, Mum," Boden called, bursting out the door after his friend.

"Be safe!" Hester called after the boys.

Jordie smiled. "Well, that settles that, then."

Hester laughed, serving them both a meal with a cup of tea. "Aye, it sure does," she said. "My son died in battle with the Orthilioans a few years back. His wife was so distraught that she killed herself, leaving three-year-old Jordan in my care."

Shocked, Jordie said, "I am so sorry."

"He is a happy lad and Lo makes sure we all have enough."

Jordie nodded. "Locryn is also good to my son."

"So, tell me a bit about yourself," Hester said, sipping her tea.

"Well," Jordie began, knowing that the truth would get out sooner or later so she might as well spill it now, "I had my son when I was young, a few months before I turned eighteen. I have been on my own, exiled from my clan ever since. Then my father turns up one day with an ultimatum to marry or else. His 'or else' was the Kedavirsta Emoratta."

Hester put her hand over her mouth. "Are you serious?"

"Very," she sighed. "My father hated me for being in love and having a babe before I was married. Shaming the family name, you know. I have learned to take care of myself."

"How long have you been on your own?"

"Seven years. Would have been eight after the new year."

"And you had to hunt and take care of yourself to survive?"

"Aye, I hunted. I never went to the clan for anything. I stayed at my cottage."

"Talking to no one?"

Jordie hung her head and nodded, "I spoke to no one for years. Well, until now. Until today and this very moment."

Hester laid her worn hand on top of Jordie's. "You poor thing," she sympathized.

Jordie shrugged. "You can only play the hand you're dealt."

Hester cocked her graying blonde head to the side. "And how do you feel about being here and married to Locryn?"

She sipped her tea, which was warm and fragrant. She drank some more of it, and before she knew it, the whole cup was gone.

"That was delicious," she said. "So far, I like it here. It feels good to be away from Veiled Hills. And Locryn is a good man."

"Good," Hester smiled. "I was surprised by the birds you brought us. Everyone is talking about it now."

Jordie narrowed her eyes. "Talking?"

"Oh, goodness, yes!" she said brightly. "They are remarking at what a fine shot you are."

Jordie seriously doubted that. If people's tongues were already wagging, and she was certain they were, it definitely wasn't about how good of a shot she was.

"How nice of them," she lied.

After that, the women talked about trivial things, and that suited Jordie just fine. It kept her from having to speak about herself. Hester opened up to her about her own life. The woman told her all about her time here with the clan, about the goings-on and other such things. For the first time in her life, Jordie wondered if she had found a friend.

There was a small silence before Jordie spoke again. "Where can I find the bath house?"

Hester looked shocked. "You want to bathe where the rest of us do?"

"Aye," she replied, "I don't want special treatment. I don't want the dresses, the soaps, the scents. I don't want the elegance, being catered to or waited on."

"Then what do you want?"

"To be accepted," Jordie said, "as an equal."

Hester smiled broadly while patting her hand. "Well, darlin' girl, you have gained me as a friend."

Jordie smiled at the older woman.

The protective part of Jordie warned her that it could all be a trick. That Hester was conniving against her, to dig up gossip and make the rumor mill fly. Maybe she wanted to tear her down and make her husband dislike her even more than he already did. However, the other part of her tried to convince her that it was all genuine. That this woman was truly kind-hearted and sweet. No matter which it happened to be, she knew that she had to deal with whatever came, however it came.

"The bathhouse is where the kitchens are, but on the inside and attached to the castle. Come," she said and held out a plate of food. "Eat along the way and I will show you."

Jordie followed Hester with her plate. Boden was playing the kicking ball game again. Merle came bounding up to her and followed at her heels.

As Hester showed her around the bath house, she explained how the stalls were made. She said that some hundred years before, an Orthilioan magic man arrived. The man magicked a drain in the middle of the bath house, sending the used water out to a rock pool by the garden. The mage wanted to craft a place where everyone could get a bath without having to wait.

Jordie's eyes widened.

There were six different cubbies and each one had a tub, a stand for linens, and soaps. It was surprisingly private with doors on the cubbies. Each stall had a trench that led to a bigger one in the middle of the bathhouse so any splashing water could get filtered out.

Hester led her to a stall in the back. Jordie looked around her in awe at the splendor and ingenuity of a chamber off the castle keep. She had never seen anything like this. Back at Veiled Hills, there was just a pool that filtered out the water and women or men would take a bath all together. Although she only took a bath with her sisters.

Hester had a bathtub filled in no time, handing her a bar of soap and some linens to dry. Merle lay down in her little cubical by the tub, watching her. Jordie set the linens down on a stool by the tub.

Jordie let out the breath she was holding, as she heard the main door shut.

"I was sure they would lock us in here together," she out loud.

Jordie tried to lock the door from the inside, but the lock was stuck and she could hear Hester telling others that she was inside using a bathing cubbie. Releasing a pent-up breath, Jordie got undressed. Her second real bath for the first time in a few days. She climbed in the high-backed copper tub, leaning her head against it with a sigh while the warm water surrounded her.

Jordie paid no attention to what was going on around her. She soaked quietly in the tub, relaxing her tired body.

"I canna believe he married a common whore!" one woman said.

"Aye, if he wanted a whore, he could o' married me!" a second woman said, laughing.

"What be that lass thinkin', tryin' ta impress us with shootin' those birds?"

"I was shocked meself," the second woman began in a pitched voice. "But she's sure manly enough ta shoot! She looked more like a man than Locryn."

Jordie sunk low in the tub, muffling out their words by putting her head under the water. The bathhouse door slammed shut, leaving her alone once again.

Hester was right. Everyone was *talking. Locryn's friends, these women, the whole damned castle. How naïve I was to think that being in a different place would allow me to be wholeheartedly accepted. I knew I wouldn't be, but part of me wished it so. And here I am, stuck forever with a man who dislikes me as much as his people do.*

Jordie squeezed her eyes tightly shut, as she floated down to the bottom of the tub, drowning everyone out.

JORDIE IN CHARGE

CHAPTER NINETEEN

*W*here *be that blasted lass?* he wondered. *I have looked all over fer her and she be nowhere. Och, she hates me that much that she snuck oot ta leave me. Damn that woman!*

He looked for her everywhere. After he kicked down her chamber door and she wasn't there, he knew she must have gone out hunting or something completely ridiculous. Now he had to find her and replace her door.

Did she not realize she didn't have to provide for herself anymore? Did she not realize that this castle had plenty of food? She didn't need to do this anymore.

He asked everyone he came across if they had seen her. But it was like she was a ghost. No one saw her leave, no one recalled her face. One woman even went as far as saying she couldn't tell his wife apart from a man.

Locryn snorted.

The guards at the iron gates saw what looked like a woman in black trews and a dark brown tunic come back in. Instantly Locryn knew that was her, but they didn't say which way she went other than she had four groewindels on her back.

All right, lass, ye didna leave, but by Corwaithe, show yer bloody face soon. We need ta clear some things up, right fuckin' now.

Becoming more frustrated, he went to the kitchens, knowing that she would take the birds there for the cook. He got there, but she wasn't there either. The head cook said a woman brought her the birds for the evening meal and then left.

He turned back around, growing more frustrated. Locryn kicked the dirt as he walked towards the stables, getting prepared to mount a horse and look for his vanished wife. Eventually, he spied Boden playing kickball with a few of the other kids.

"Mum is back, don't worry," was all the boy said before running off with Jordan and a few other lads.

That bloody blasted eejit o' a lass, he cursed. *I be goin' ta spank her arse till it be so red she wilna be able ta sit down fer a damned week!*

Locryn was tremendously irate at the point.

Drensent was a massive castle with many places to hide. He went inside the castle, looking for her, stupidly calling her name. He looked all over the bloody keep, checking in all the places her small self could hide.

Still no Jordie.

It wasn't until he wandered aimlessly around the castle yard, when he saw the kindly cook Hester. She was the type of person who befriended everything and everyone. That was when he finally discovered her whereabouts. The bathhouse.

190

Jordie was supposed to stay in her room. Although he didn't make his wishes clear, she was supposed to be there, unpacking her things. His mother kindly ordered her a bath and she wasn't there to receive it. And already his mother was furious, not only at him, but at the disrespect from her new daughter.

Locryn himself was furious but over different reasons.

She had gone out into the wild all by herself, telling no one. She had made his mother upset and cry. She made chaos out of everything. She didn't have the decency to tell him anything. Jordie was being rude and uncivilized. And this behavior was ending today, right damned now!

He went to the bathhouse, assuming she would still be there. Locryn rounded the corner to the find the door open and no one inside. He checked each cubical. His wife wasn't there.

"Damn her!" he yelled. "Damn that fuckin', sneaky-arsed woman!"

Hester came up beside him. "Lo, don't be mad at her," she told him placatingly. "A few of the girls were talking, said some unkind things, opened the door to her cubical and took her clothes. So, she left."

Locryn turned on her. "Where did she go?"

Hester motioned outside. "Back to her room in the West Tower."

Locryn ran out of the castle kitchens, bounding up the West Tower stairs two at a time. Sure enough, there she was, standing in the middle of her room, a giant linen towel around her. And also, sure enough, her weapons were on the bed.

She had been crying, her face pointed towards the floor as he burst in. "I thought it was someone come to bring me something to wear. So, I left the door open," she told him, staring at her feet. "They took my clothes and ran."

"So ye came back here?" he asked, his anger just slightly dissipating.

Jordie nodded. "Where was I to go?"

He was still mad at her, but now, not so much. Still she had no right to go outside the Drensent walls, doing what she did. She had no right to come and go as she pleased without an escort, without telling him or someone else. All of his previous anger came back.

"Me mother had ordered ye a bath," he told her seriously.

She looked at him, face emboldened. "I do not wish to be catered to."

"Damn it, Jordie! Yer me wife. Yer the heir's wife! Ye will be catered ta. As I have told ye befer, lass, ye will do what I say!"

He could tell she was overwhelmed and frustrated, but he needed to let her know her place. Things were different now. She couldn't do everything all on her own and, abyss to it all, she was going to get used to it!

"Yer no' ta leave here withoot me any longer. Yer no' ta go huntin' and yer certainly no' allowed ta wear men's clothes. This changes here and now!"

Jordie's face turned red with fury. "I wish to leave here then!"

Locryn scowled back, "Oh, ye do now?"

"Aye, I do, and I will—as you so promised me."

"Despise me that much, do ye?"

Jordie rolled her eyes, folding her arms across the towel that covered her body. "You're the one who doesn't care for me! So why should I stay somewhere when no one wants me? It's clear that you don't, neither does your family or this clan."

"Ye never even gave me a chance, lass!" Locryn spat back.

Jordie angrily strode towards him, pointing a finger at his chest and clutching the towel with the other. "My name is Jordie, and neither did you!" she yelled. "You only assumed what you cared to know. You have shown it at every turn. By the revulsion on your face and the way you carry yourself around me. I could be the holiest of women yet, once your mind is set, there is no turning it around. And I do not wish to constantly prove myself to you."

Locryn was quiet, fists clenching and unclenching, but before he could speak, she continued, "Do you think I am so senseless to not notice the way your mother spoke to me? The way your friends look at me? The way they talk about me when they think I'm not around? I was able to get past you as your one friend said, 'Ye better dump the lass like a burnt cake.'" She shook her head. "I have the same bullshit here as I did at Veiled Hills. So, aye, I don't want to be your wife. I want to be on my own."

193

Locryn's anger was rising to the point of breaking. He had tried for days to talk to her, but she didn't speak back. He had tried to soften up toward her, to accept her as she was. But he found that he couldn't.

Finn was right when he said that he had married Jordie out of pity. He did take pity on her. On her hard life, on her struggles, on everything. But he was now coming to think that she struggled so much for a reason, and that reason being was that Jordie was a whore.

Her family did right to cast her out of Veiled Hills, her family was right to not speak to her, her clan was right to ignore her. And here he was, stupid enough to fall for her alluring amber eyes, pink pouty lips, and her determined, tenacious nature. He was stupid to fall for the loving, caring nature she exuded.

"Fine," he said, "Come with me."

He grabbed her wrist in a vise. He dragged her out of the West Tower, across the castle grounds, through the mud in her bare feet, and to an abandoned cottage out in the back. He opened the rotting door. It creaked as he shoved her inside.

"Stay here as ye were befer. Dinna come in the keep or in the tower. Dinna look fer me. Dinna say me name. We're done," he slammed the door on her, shaking the whole place. "The priest will be back in a few weeks from visitin' the nearby villages, then we will end this marriage. I be done with ye, Jordie Duvoir. Ye dinna deserve me last name, ye whore!"

194

•••••

Jordie stood there in the middle of the shack. She didn't know what to say. Aye, she wanted to be free. She also wanted to love and be loved, but once again, it was clear that it wasn't meant to be.

Another piece of her heart shattered. For some reason, crying came easier to her as of late, but she couldn't bring herself to do it now. Tears solved nothing. Tears made the emotions a little less painful to deal with, but in the end, they solved nothing. The linen towel was still wrapped around her. If she was careful, she could turn it into a new pair of trews for Boden.

Jordie turned away from the door, scanning the dusty old place, looking for anything of general use. She found a pair of boots which were much too small for her feet. She found a few tunics. The dark green one was thick, and she put it on to block out the winter's cold.

The weather certainly turned fast this far north. The sun wasn't yet making its way towards the east to set, for there were still a few hours of daylight left, but the coldness of winter was certainly creeping in. She dug around some more until she found trews which were fortunately just her size. Whoever had previously lived or died here, she was thankful for their things.

Someone came up to her cottage, their bulky shadow evident through the cracks on the door. The person set something down and walked away. She knew it was her small chest of clothing, quilt, and dining ware.

195

She braided her hair off to the side, waiting for the person to leave. The booted footfalls faded quickly. Quietly, she went to open the door. It was the first thing she needed to fix, but she couldn't afford the nails. She brought in her chest and her son's. Her pair of boots sat on top of it all.

Jordie opened the three windows, letting the sun and cold air into the musty home. She opened her trunk to find the small sack of coins Locryn had on his person when he was out getting her son sugared buns and new boots.

She opened it to find four silver coins and fifteen coppers. It would be enough to get a new door at least. If she was careful, this could last her a few years.

Jordie paused, hearing boots.

Jordie opened the door again, this time to find her bow, arrows, her hatchet, and three knives. Like a thief, she snatched it all hurriedly. She closed the door behind her, fastening all her weapons to her person and walked boldly to the middle of town where her son was before.

Sure enough, he was still there, playing the kicking ball game with his friends. She held up her bow, which Boden nodded and went back out into the forest to hunt for some dinner for themselves now.

The guards were lax, letting her past, but not before calling out a warning to her that they close the gates to all when the moon began to rise at night. She waved a hand and walking past them, hoping to see something other than a groewindel. She had almost three hours until dark.

She looked back only once to see Locryn on the outer wall, glowering down at her. She couldn't keep the hurt from her face as she looked back at him. Jordie turned around and kept walking on into the forest. He made up his mind about her days ago. There was no going back now.

He could never have loved me, anyway, she thought. *It was never meant to be.*

JORDIE IN CHARGE

CHAPTER TWENTY

H e watched her leave under the portcullis, going back out into the cold forest. He was thrilled he never got her a ring. She didn't deserve it. She wouldn't have appreciated it, anyway.

He was so angry with himself for letting himself be suckered into marriage. She made him feel sorry for her. She made him want to take her in. She made him want to love her long into the night and wake up to her, lying naked beside him, wholly satisfied in the morning.

Jordie was a witch!

And her father knew it. No wonder he called for an Emoratta. And Locryn was the stupid shit to look past it all, feeling sorry for this silly, ridiculous, vehement woman. Jordie was everything a woman shouldn't be—wild, strong-willed, self-reliant, stubborn, and rude.

"Damn her!" he yelled. "Damn that bloody woman."

"Damn her, huh?" said a taller man coming up alongside of him, carrying a sleeping babe in one arm.

Locryn looked at the small babe, wrapped up tight in a pink quilted blanket. "She be a such bonny lass, Laird Thomas."

"Aye, and so be yer wife, brother."

Locryn scowled and as Jordie disappeared behind the tall trees. "She be no' me wife anymore."

Thomas snorted.

"Ye doubt me?"

Thomas turned his back, leaning against the stone. "She be yer wife, Locryn. Ye married her."

Locryn turned red in the face, "She be no' what she seems."

The wise laird shook his head. "Ye fool! O' course no'. She had ta defend herself, provide fer herself. She had no one ta love her, ta be there fer her. Time and loneliness shaped her. I ken her story. I also ken the man she loved."

Locryn turned on his brother in shock. "Ye ken the man?"

Thomas nodded, rocking the babe in his arms, "Aye, Lane Flashew was the man she loved. Left her right after he promised her forever." Thomas looked sadly in the direction in which she went. "I went ta that new tavern in Norgeral fer an ale—no' too bad, by the way—and there he be. Boastin' in a corner table about how he tricked the laird's daughter and left her pregnant, alone in the woods. Tellin' her family that she trapped him and that she be a whore." Thomas shook his head. "Tellin' anyone who would listen her name. Then told everyone how the family paid him handsomely fer all his poor misery and made him leave. Lane was laughin' when he got ta the part where her family cast her oot."

Locryn deflated. "I did no' ken, brother.

"Remember when I courted Ehlowen and her family tried ta tell me she be a horrid lass? Remember how they lied and tried ta cast her in a poor light, but she never did anythin' wrong?"

"I do remember that."

"Aye, and Ehlowen be no' horrid, be she?"

"Nay, she be a right good woman."

Thomas patted his younger brother on the shoulder. "Dinna be an eejit. Jordie may have had a child, but she be no' a horrid woman. We might be only a few years apart, but I got all the smarts." Thomas winked and walked away.

Locryn sighed.

He watched the trees in the distance for any sign of his wife. He stared off in the direction she went, wondering if she would come back soon. Locryn kicked the stone.

Damn it all, he cursed.

He walked back down the wall walk, heading to her ramshackle place he put her in. Without a moment's hesitation, he began moving her things back up into his chamber, now theirs. Her trunk was still surprisingly light and he never understood why she kept the things she had until now. It was because of him. It was because he hadn't learned to trust her. And he didn't do as Aramoren said—to help her trust.

Locryn opened the bedroom door and slid her trunk across the floor. He looked at his chamber with the eyes of a married man. Would this bachelor's pad be good enough for his Jordie? Locryn stepped inside, picking up the tunics and trews dropped on the floor. Then he went to get Boden.

"Let's get ye some new clothes, aye?" Locryn said.

"Really?" Boden asked, Merle hopping at his side.

"Aye, really," Locryn said. "Ye need better ones than what ye have on. Ye can wear those fer play."

Boden beamed at the man. "Thank ye, Da."

When they arrived at the seamstress's quarters, Locryn handed the woman coin and told her what he wanted for his son to wear. He also asked for a little something else from her stores. Willa came back and handed him what he asked for. She always had extra clothes made.

Locryn left his son in Willa's capable hands and headed back up to the wall to look for his wife. As he looked in every direction, he thought about everything Thomas had said about Jordie. And he knew Thomas was right.

Time and loneliness shaped her into what she was today. She had thrived without him. She had done so much without him. By Corwaithe, he even judged her, like she knew he would, like she said that he would and did. Still, she didn't even bat an eyelash to it. On top of it all, she called him out on what he was doing to her.

He hadn't taken the time to hear her side. To defend her from gossiping tongues, to protect her from the words from even his friends. He scowled at her. He looked at her with something akin to hate and disgust. He was wrong about her and now he called her a whore.

Abyss, she didn't even cry!

She didn't even twitch at the most hurtful word he could call a woman. Jordie didn't even make a remark when he said that she didn't deserve his last name. She stood there before him, taking it all in like she had done for years. Bottling it up and suppressing it for another seven years.

And everyone heard him call her so. And everyone watched as he publicly shamed his wife by leaving her in that shack.

Locryn hung his head.

It was she who didn't deserve him. He hadn't even give her a chance. She was right about that. She kept quiet, while the screaming inside his head made him believe the absolute worst of her.

He didn't stop his friends from saying what they did, for he too felt the same way. He let his mother bully her. By all rights, she had the right to ask him to leave her alone. It was, after all, what he promised her. And he had always thought of himself as a man of integrity.

"Hello, Lo," a female voice said.

His bonny sister-in-law came up beside him. Queen Ehlowen was the voice of reason. She was the only person he knew who didn't judge anyone or say an unkind word. Ehlowen was as pure as a blooming spring flower. She always had something nice to say.

"I have yet to meet your new wife," she said, her honey hair braided and curled around her angelic head.

"She be oot at the moment."

203

Ehlowen placed a hand on his arm. "Out where? Out in this cold?"

"Aye," he nodded. "She be oot huntin' because I be an ass."

"I see. And what have you done to stop her?"

He sighed, "No' a damned thing."

He could talk to Ehlowen about anything, mainly because she refused to cast condemnation. Occasionally, she would ask a question but offer no advice, and always end with a smile and some sort of final statement that left him thinking.

She was a mystery that Thomas got lucky enough to find. They were good for each other and part of him was envious of what they happened to share together. They had been together for many years, since Thomas was twenty-two and she eighteen. Now they finally had their first child eight years later and a second on the way.

He stood there on the parapet, looking down over his clan's territory. He told his sister-in-law everything that had happened in the past few days. The cold started to set in and everywhere around him smoke billowed from the chimneys of homes. People were settling in for the night, carrying their loads of firewood or gathering their children since the light of day was now just a shimmer.

There was going to be a feast tonight to honor him and his wife. His whole clan would be there to celebrate. The cooks would serve the beasts that she shot down earlier this afternoon. Jordie's generosity helped the clan immensely.

But while the clan prepared to make merry, Jordie was still out there, hunting. Her son would be worried, but Boden knew his mother would be back. He was the only thing she would come back for.

Och, but I've been such a dummy, as she had called him once.

He had moved their things out into that drafty, old, deteriorating-to-piss cottage. And she never even complained one bit as he dragged her out to it. He had gripped her so tightly he was sure it would leave a bruise. And he did all of this while she was in nothing but a damn piece of linen she used as a towel.

When she looked back at him as she went out into those woods, oh how he would never forget her gorgeous face. The sadness in her eyes, the hurt, the sorrow of her heart there. She looked back only once before going out of his view. She wanted him to appreciate her for who she was and instead he hated her for it.

"What is she worth to you?" Ehlowen asked after many moments of silence.

"What d'ye mean?"

"What is her value to you? A silver coin? A golden chalice? Everything or nothing at all?"

He looked at her confused. "I dinna ken."

She looked at him pitifully, but before she walked away, she said, "Don't compare an apple to an orange. They are both different and beautiful, each having a purpose and a worth."

Then she made her way down the stone steps to go back inside the castle. When he looked back, he spied his wife coming through the gates. She didn't look up at him. She kept walking with her head down and a broeshilak in her hand, headed toward her home.

The shack he had shoved her into.

CHAPTER TWENTY-ONE

She saw him up there, watching the forest for her, scanning it whenever that beautiful woman wasn't talking to him directly. That was who he needed—someone beautiful, obedient, and quiet. Someone so passive, it was silly. And that person wasn't her.

Jordie knew that he saw her. She could feel his piercing blue eyes upon her. He was watching her every move, her every step as she made her way back to the home that was now hers and hers alone. A new home in which she would make the best place she could for her son.

Grumpily, she marched back to her house. She opened the damaged door, letting it swing shut as she put down the broeshilak on the rough table. She began skinning the animal, working quickly while the blood was still warm.

Where was that son of hers? He should be here by now. She wiped her hands off on her tunic before setting out to find Boden. Jordie didn't have to go far, for there he was, coming out of the West Tower.

"Look, Mum!" he called, bounding up to her. "Da got me new clothes."

"Careful, Boden," she cautioned, "I have blood on my clothes."

"You're the best hunter ever," he said. Then spinning he said, "What do you think?"

"You look wonderful, Boden," she said. "Very handsome."

"Are you coming, Mum?"

"Coming to what?"

"Comin' ta the feast, lass," Locryn called out behind her.

She didn't respond. She glared at him instead. The last thing he told her was not to come to the keep, which meant no feast for her, thankfully.

"Ye goin' ta talk ta me?" he asked her.

Jordie rolled her eyes. "You told me not to."

"I was wrong," he said. "Will ye come ta the feast tonight?"

She turned around to face her husband, her eyes bright with fury. Was he going to be different this time around or was he going to spray more foul things out of his supposedly noble mouth?

"Nay," she said shaking her head, "I don't want to go."

"Why no'?"

"I do not wish to be humiliated," she replied, crossing her arms and standing in front of her son.

He came closer and she backed away.

He was going to have to prove himself to her. She wanted him to want her, like how she wanted a life and a family. And at the same time, she wanted him, she wanted him to leave forever. It was like the dark side of the moon: to want to see it, but at the same time to be terrified to know what the other side had to offer.

Locryn looked down at his feet and when he looked up, his translucent blue eyes pierced hers. "Ye wilna be humiliated, Jordie."

"Are you making me another promise, Locryn?"

He reached for her small hand. "Aye, I be makin' ye a promise."

Jordie pulled her hand away. "And how do I know you'll keep it without being spiteful?"

"Will ye trust me, lass?"

She looked at his handsome face.

He looked sincere. He looked remorseful. But he should be for what he had said and done. Her husband had condemned her a thousand times over. Now he wanted her to trust him. Again. He called her something no husband should ever call a wife, even if it were true. But he did, and it hurt so much more coming from the lips of her husband than it did from anyone else.

Could she trust him?

How? How can I trust him again?

He reached for her hand again. This time she let him take it.

"Trust me, lass . . . please," he begged.

She looked into his gentle blue eyes and then down at her son, who grinned.

She sighed, "This one last time, Locryn."

He smiled sincerely. "Thank ye, lass."

"But I am not kidding around. I deserve better," she said, tears stinging in her eyes. "And my damn name is Jordie!"

Locryn moved close to her, inches from her body, "I wilna hurt ye."

So, you have said before, she thought.

She still didn't trust him, but for better or for worse, she wanted to. He got her and her son out of that abyss pit back home. And he loved Boden as if he were his own, buying him boots and clothes and spending hours talking to the boy.

"I moved yer things back in," he said.

Back in where, she wondered, *and how? I wasn't gone very long.*

She didn't want to stay with him, even though they were married. If she did, he might make her stop hunting, stop working, and start wearing those awful confining dresses.

He silently led her up the stairs, past her door, and all the way to the top, to where his room was. Her heart began to race. Locryn opened the door for her.

Jordie stepped inside, seeing his chamber for the first time. It was a large bedroom with a hearth off to the right and directly across from it was his four-poster bed. Two cushioned chairs sat before the fire with a small table in the middle.

Her trunk waited right in front of her with something folded and tied with ribbon.

Locryn took her hand. "Please stay," he whispered.

Jordie turned around to Boden, who followed behind them. "Go to the feast, love. We will be following shortly."

"Aye, Mum," said Boden. "I was going to say something because I am starving!" he said and bounded down the stairs.

Jordie turned an inquisitive brow at her husband. "Spontaneous change of heart, huh?"

She crossed her arms and waited for him to say something. He looked forlorn but she wasn't going to give him any quarter. She didn't want an apology. She didn't want an explanation. What she wanted was for him to own what he did.

"I should have believed ye," he said.

"Aye, you should have," she said. "I have nothing to gain by lying to you about my past, you know. But how am I to trust you now?"

"I be sorry, Jordie," he breathed out roughly, "I should no' have said that."

Tears stung her eyes. "Nay, you shouldn't have," she said angrily.

"Och, wife, dinna cry," he said, wiping a tear from her face. "I wilna hurt ye again, this I so swear ta ye."

211

She pulled away, shaking her head. "You don't understand," she told him. "You hurt me! I trusted you. I stupidly believed that you were different and that I was going to have a good life, not only for myself but for my son. But we aren't even divorced yet and you were with a different woman."

•••••

He was even more confused. Tears welled in her eyes and her lips trembled. He didn't even know what it was over, other than the little clues she gave. He hurt her with his insults. He hurt her by thinking the worst of her, over what her father did, and now she somehow though he'd been with another woman.

"Wait," he said as clarity dawned on him. "Ye saw Ehlowen up on the wall with me today, aye?"

Jordie nodded.

"Och, she be me brother Thomas's wife."

"See," she cried, "I really am stupid."

Locryn pulled her close, her hot, tear-stained face against his chest. She struck his chest, but he held her fast, soothing her with kind words and stroking her hair. She put her hands in fists on his chest, trying rather poorly to keep him away from her.

He looked down at her, but she hid her face in his chest. Jordie was trying so hard not to give into him. And suddenly he realized how badly he hurt her.

For seven long years, she lived alone. For seven long years, she endured cruelty from clan and family. By herself, she birthed and raised her child. And here she thought she had finally found a person to confide in, to love—and he had betrayed her.

He mistakenly hurt this beautiful, caring, capable woman. This woman in his arms was falling apart at the seams.

"Yer no' an eejit, Jordie," he said, cupping her red face. "I be so verra sorry I didna believe ye in the first place."

She laughed, "And you figured this out *now*?"

"I be an eejit too. We all have our moments o' no' bein' verra keen."

"Aye, I cannot disagree there," she smiled.

Locryn kissed her forehead. "Start over with me, Jordie?" he asked her, pulling her face towards his and looking into her eyes.

•••••

Start over? Are there such simple things? she had to wonder. *Is he even real? Can a warring man, a king's son, a powerful heir, want to start over with me? Or is this another deceptive hope?*

"Start over with me," he said again.

Jordie looked him in the eyes, searching for the lie. But she didn't see anything other than regret and compassion.

213

Jordie nodded.

Locryn kissed her forehead, warm and soft. He still held her close, his strong arms wrapped around her. Burying her face in his chest, she breathed in his heady scent. She felt her walls crumbling as he held her, her defenses slipping away as he pressed his lips against her head again. His massive calloused hand tangled itself in her hair as the other hand spilled warmth on her back.

For the first time in a very long time, she felt secure and safe. Instead of fighting him, she embraced his comfort. Jordie laid her head on his shoulder, wrapping her arms around his muscular torso.

Locryn held her there. His large arms wrapped around her tightly. He stroked her hair and rubbed her back. Jordie relaxed, closing her eyes and relishing the quiet moment. She took it all in, just in case it happened to disappear again.

Jordie sighed, her eyes closed, breathing in the scent that was her husband.

She pulled away slightly to look in his eyes. "Is it all that simple?" she asked, worrying, wondering.

He grinned. "Still weighin' all possible options, I see."

"We are married after all," she began.

"Aye, we be married."

"Treat me as an equal?" she asked with a flirtatious quirk of her eyebrow.

He pulled her in close and kissed the top of her dark red head again. "If ye start tellin' me how ye feel instead o' keepin' it all in, then aye."

214

She gave him a genuine smile. "Deal."

"I be goin' ta check on our son," he said as he went to the door. "I hope that," he pointed to the folded package tied with ribbon, "fits ye."

JORDIE IN CHARGE

CHAPTER TWENTY-TWO

After Locryn left, Jordie took a peek around her new room. She walked around his chamber, touching the things that he owned, which were mostly weapons.

She opened the wardrobe doors and all of Locryn's clothes came out like a waterfall. Jordie closed her eyes and smiled.

I see this is something that never changes, she thought. *Even when they get older, they are still slobs.*

Neatly, she folded everything and put it away. She rolled his belts together, placing them on the bottom of the wooden shelf. Jordie walked around, picking up weapons and putting them in sheaths, then inside the wardrobe as well. She hung the rest on the wardrobe doors.

Jordie stood in the middle of the room, looking around at what else she could pick up, but there was nothing. The fire in the hearth was warm and inviting, calling to her to sit and rest. But she couldn't.

Jordie walked over to a small table with a bowl that was just behind the door. A big bowl full of water and a couple of wash clothes and a towel were beside it with a bar of soap sitting on top. Jordie glanced at herself in a mirror and frowned.

I cannot go looking like this, she thought.

Jordie took off her trews, looking down at her legs. They were for the most part clean, but Jordie found a washcloth and basin and scoured soap into the linen.

There wasn't enough time to take another bath before the feast. So, she scrubbed herself as best she could and then attacked the rest of her naked body. By the time she was done, the water basin was tinged red and brown, evidence of her hunting.

She walked naked over to the package sitting on top of her trunk. With delicate hands, she pulled at the ribbon bow and unwrapped the paper, taking her time and appreciating what Locryn went through to do this for her. Pushing aside the paper, she found cloth inside and lifted up its edges.

Jordie's eyes widened.

A beautiful blue gown with lace trim in the sleeves greeted her eyes. Under the gown were matching blue leather slippers. Jordie felt tears well up in her eyes.

"D'ye like it, Jordie?" Locryn said from behind her.

Jordie turned around, not at all startled by her husband seeing her naked backside. A broad smile creased her lips.

"Aye, I love it," she told him. "Thank you."

Locryn nodded. "I will wait ootside the door fer ye."

He shut the door behind himself. Jordie pulled the slippers on her feet, then stepped into the dress. Jordie tied the stays in the front. She spun in a circle, seeing the fabric swirl around her.

She looked in the mirror again and gasped. She had never looked so lovely, not even as a princess in Veiled Hills. The blue brought out her sun-kissed color. Her eyes sparkled in the firelight.

Her hands went to her hair, wondering what to do about her long, tangled, messy locks. Jordie combed her hands through her hair since she didn't have a brush. She tilted her head to the side, starting the braid at the top of her head and working her way back in a zig-zag pattern. When she finished, the braid ended on the left side of her face.

It will have to do, I suppose, she sighed. *At least I don't smell like dead animal.*

When she opened the door, Locryn turned around. A wide smile split his face as he took her arm. Jordie smiled up at him.

"Is it all right?" she asked.

Locryn nodded, kissing the back of her hand. "More than all right. Ye look stunnin'."

•••••

The feast was something grand. Everything she hadn't tasted in years was put in front of her. Everything she could ever desire was right there and Locryn loaded it all on her plate. He smiled at her whenever he added something new. She couldn't help but laugh and smile back.

Mutton, beef, garlic and peppercorn rolls, soup, gravy and so much more were all at one point on her wooden plate. She had never eaten so much in her life, but every bite tasted so good that it had the possibility of being her absolute last. She was gulping it down, hardly chewing, but taking appropriate bites since she was in public view. Locryn sat beside her in awe of how much she put away.

"Slow down, Jordie," Locryn said.

"I don't want for this to end," she replied before biting into another roll.

"Wife, it wilna end. There be food tomorrow as well and every meal after that."

She grinned back at him. "Aye, well, I need to get used to this then."

"Aye, ye do," he said, chuckling.

She smiled at him, enjoying this easy, happy moment. Boden was a few tables over, sitting with a group of other young lads and his new best friend, Jordan. He was talking merrily, and for once in her life, she didn't have to worry if he had enough to eat.

Then she wasn't hungry anymore.

Jordie paused, looking at her plate of food, then to her satisfied son. She would never have to be worried about food again. Never again would she fear famine sinking its cruel teeth into her family.

She dared a glance at Locryn, who was looking at her with an inquisitive brow. She stared down at her food.

"What be the matter, Jordie?"

We agreed to be honest with each other, she thought.

"We've never had this much food."

Locryn strummed his fingers on the table. "Did ye ever go hungry?"

Her head hung low. She didn't answer.

"Aye," she finally said, looking at him with grim seriousness, "I went without. I would never let Boden starve."

Locryn leaned forward and took her hand in his two warm ones. "No' ever again," he vowed to her.

She smiled at him.

She had never just stopped and looked at him before. He was different now, or mayhap she was. Or mayhap they both were. On the way here, she'd glared at him and punished him with silence. She didn't appreciate the man for who he truly was.

Now she saw him in a new light. He was kind to her, caring to her and Boden, making sure they both had enough on their plates. Already Boden had new clothes and she didn't have to scramble to sell something for fabric.

Everything they needed was right there.

He was right there.

Locryn smiled at her and rubbed her back, putting another slice of groewindel on her plate.

Jordie reached under the table with her left hand and put it on his leg. She looked at him with appreciation. She was wrong about him, as he was about her, but now, together, they could start over.

CHAPTER TWENTY-THREE

The feast went on for a while longer before the plates were cleared and dessert was brought out. Sugared buns, chocolate confections, and fluffy cakes. There were so many things to devour and she was in heaven. Her son scarfed everything down just as quickly as she did. Jordie knew he would have a stomachache later for she already felt hers coming on.

She savored every bite of the chocolate wiggly thing that Locryn called mousse. She had never seen it before in her life. It was never at Veiled Hills but she loved it. Then he put a white fluffy cake in front of her, which she devoured just as quickly as the mousse. Although it wasn't as delicious, she couldn't help but eat two slices.

Jordie was having such a wonderful time eating, being merry, and sitting close to her husband. They were getting along better now that there was an understanding. She felt confident within herself. They each gave each other an ultimatum and they each had the choice to follow it. And mayhap someday in the future, the ultimatum would be forgotten, but for right now, it was the single piece gluing them together.

"How wonderful," the former reigning queen said. "Yer here and all cleaned up, I see."

Jordie didn't remark on that.

She focused on her plate. It was something her husband should handle; after all, this was his mother and his clan. She had yet to gain the clan's acceptance on her own.

"She be me wife, mother," Locryn reminded her. "She be no' goin' anywhere."

"Oh," Julia commented, "then I assume that what I heard earlier be incorrect?"

Locryn knew what his mother was getting at. "Mother," he said, voice low and deadly, "stop it."

"I just be merely askin', son," she feigned. "I just want her ta feel welcome and have her stay be nice and comfortable."

"Mother," Thomas interjected, "That be enough."

Jordie looked up from her plate to stare daggers at her new mother-in-law. She was going to have a battle on her hands with her. But Jordie wasn't going to back down. This woman, whether she liked it or not, was going to respect her.

"With all due respect," Jordie said, "do you have something on your mind you wish to say to my face?"

Locryn placed a hand on her shoulder, warning her, but she knew what she was doing. If there was going to be peace, then things needed to be said. Here or somewhere else, now or later, words were going to be said.

Locryn got up from the table, taking both women by the arm and leading them to the laird's study, Thomas's room, on the bottom floor.

Julia swept into the study first and then rounded on Jordie.

"Do ye truly wish ta ken?" she said.

"Nothing you can ever say will even come close to the cruel things my family has said to me and the things I have experienced. So, do your worst, if you will."

Julia sneered, "Yer a whore, and me son, fer some cursed reason, decided ta be married ta ye. I dinna want ye here. No one does. I would prefer it if ye left."

"I see," Jordie said. "And do you care to hear the other side of the story?"

Julia laughed. "Foolish woman, there be no need."

"So, the *former* queen deems it wise to pass judgements without all the facts."

"How dare ye!" Julia hissed.

"Oh, I dare," she smiled sweetly. "For I have been lied to, stomped on, betrayed, thrown out, and left to fend for myself on my own. Nothing you will ever say will hurt me. Take your words somewhere else, for they fall on deaf ears."

Jordie walked out and slammed the door on Julia's shrill insults, letting Locryn deal with his mother. What Jordie really wanted to do was laugh. From the moment she met the nasty woman, Jordie had been respectful and kind.

But evidently, Julia did not like being put in her place or being told the truth.

Jordie stood outside the door a moment, listening to Julia complain. Jordie rolled her eyes at the ridiculous accusations. Julia seemed to be making up stories about what Jordie did, what she said, and where she went, and none of it was true. But, bless Corwaithe, Locryn knew exactly where she was: out hunting.

Julia was still arguing as Jordie walked back to the dining hall alone. She sat in her chair with a rigid back, watching her son. Today was the first day he could freely play and chat with others. Where he could eat whatever he wanted and however much he wanted. Where he was accepted by friends. She couldn't ruin that for him.

She began to look around at all the other tables. There were so many people in the dining hall. She hadn't noticed it before. In front of her, were at least thirty people to a table, if not more, and at least ten or more tables and so many benches. It amazed her. This clan was so much bigger than Veiled Hills ever was. And there was still room for more tables if there needed to be.

Everyone was chatting and being merry. She knew it wasn't because of the fact that their laird's brother was married. The wedding was simply a reason to get together and eat. Occasionally, her clansmen would point at her with serious expressions on their faces. She could only speculate at what they were saying.

What she really wanted to do was call them all out. Ask them why they glared, sneered, and gossiped about her, when in truth they all had no clue about her life. But she couldn't make them understand something they didn't want to, so in the end, there was no point in calling them out on their prattling garbage.

Jordie sighed. She was tired of the conversing, the listening, the scowls and jeers, but because of her son, she put up with it. Anything to see him smile. Anything to see him laugh with his friends.

Finally, Locryn returned, but he sat staring down at his lap.

"Something wrong?" she ventured to ask.

"Aye."

"Care to tell me what it is?"

Locryn lifted his head and glared into her dark amber eyes. "If I stay married ta ye, Julia will make it so we divorce. Me Grandpa Bellamy will assist and she will force Thomas inta this as well, ta make ye leave."

Jordie's heart sunk.

She knew what she had to do, what she had to say. There were so many forces working against her. She had known it all along. This marriage was something of a false hope from the start. It was just a flickering light in a never-ending tunnel of despair.

Jordie looked deep into his amazing blue eyes, then nodded. "All right then. Where is the divorce paper?"

JORDIE IN CHARGE

CHAPTER TWENTY-FOUR

"Ye canna be serious, Jordie," Locryn said, rising to his feet in front of everyone. "We be married. That's it! As Corwaithe says, this be forever."

Jordie rose to her feet, not backing down. "Aye, but I don't want your good name to be run through the mud."

Locryn towered over her. "Yer me wife, Jordie. That be it."

Jordie growled, "You're willing to lose your family, home, money, and clan for me?" She sighed and put a hand over her face. "You don't even know that much about me."

"I ken enough about ye ta ken I married ye and that I love ye!"

"Cut the shit, Locryn!" she yelled, taking a step towards him. "I will not let you become an outcast in your own home and clan!"

She knew everyone was watching.

His mother, the clan, everyone had gone completely silent. It wasn't a good feeling she was having. She hated the echoing silence. It was unnerving. Everyone was judging her at this moment. Judging them both. Listening to every word so they could talk about it later.

She just couldn't let Locryn throw away his life. His wonderful life. As his wife, she wouldn't let him ruin what he had going for him. It wasn't fair. It wasn't right. Married or not, people made sacrifices for each other, but this was too much.

Jordie wouldn't allow him to do this. Not for her. Not for her son. Locryn had done enough for them already in getting them away from Veiled Hills, for giving her son boots and clothes, for giving them food to eat and a roof over their heads. He had done enough.

"Yer me wife. I make the decisions," he said.

She snorted. "We haven't consummated anything, so if you want to get all technical, this could be null and void really quick."

"Who says we haven't?"

"You, sir, are a special kind of stupid!"

"Oh, I be stupid, aye?"

"Aye!"

"Then tell me why I be such a numptie in yer hallowed eyes, Jordie."

Jordie crossed her arms, glaring at him in frustration. "Have you learned nothing while being at Veiled Hills? Did you not see what I experienced or did you turn a blind eye to the obvious?"

"I saw what happened."

"Then please give me a damn good reason why you would want that for yourself? Why you would want to live forever as an outcast—unaccepted, hated, humiliated, shunned—for the rest of your life? Wouldn't you want better for yourself?"

"Yer me wife, and that be reason enough!"

"Well," she sighed, "I am ending this, for your own good."

"Fer me own good?"

"Aye!" she yelled, "Because I like you enough to do what is right even if you're too thick to do it."

"I'm thick?"

"Holy Goddess!" she swore. "Yes, for goodness sake, yes! Please take a moment to pull your head out of your ass! I care about you! I care about you a lot to do what must be done! I love you enough to let you go."

Snickers from the men echoed throughout the room. For a moment, she had forgotten they were there. From the look on Locryn's face, so did he. His face turned red; his body trembled with rage. For the first time in her life, she was terrified for herself, but she knew he wouldn't strike her. He wasn't that kind of man.

She wasn't going to flinch. Jordie stood her ground. Everyone watched. Their waiting eyes heated her cheeks with embarrassment. Her knees wanted to knock together, but she stopped them.

This must be what it felt like to meet him in battle, she thought.

"I love you enough to do what is right," she said.

Locryn's nostrils flared. "We be no'," he growled so low that it vibrated her bones, "gettin' a divorce."

Jordie came within inches of his face, lowering her voice, but she knew everyone still heard. "Then you will curse the day you married me because of it!"

And she walked away. She stopped at Boden's table to gather him, and together they went to the West Tower. She had to explain to Boden what was to come. This would be the hardest thing she was ever going to have to do.

•••••

They walked back to his room in silence. Boden's face was sad. He must have figured some of it out. After all, he was a smart lad. He trudged up the stairs, looking down and saying nothing.

Jordie opened the door for her son, who entered sullenly. Methodically, he removed his clothes to put on a night tunic. Jordie had never felt so guilty. She had to tell him her reasons why she wanted to divorce his father. It would just crush her son, for he so adored the man.

Boden gathered his clothes, putting them in a pile for tomorrow. Next, he picked up Merle and climbed into his new warm bed. And as she watched him, her heart fell further. This was the first time he ever had something so luxurious all to himself, and it was something as simple as actual bed.

Jordie tucked the blankets up under his chin, stroking the hair out of his face. She kissed him on the forehead, relishing his sweet innocent face.

"Boden," she began, "I know how much you adore Da."

It was so hard to see the look on his face. The confusion and pain. He didn't understand, but she had to explain things in some way. All his life, Boden had suffered from the way people treated her. And now it happened yet again.

Jordie sighed. "Sometimes, you have to do what is right, even though it may hurt so bad."

"You like Da, right, Mum?"

"Aye, I do. I like him a lot."

Boden sat up in bed, hands together. "Then why?"

She sighed. "Remember when no one talked to us? Remember how hard it was to do things sometimes? For me to go to town?"

Boden nodded.

"Would you want Da to feel the same way you or I did?"

Boden shook his head.

Jordie cupped his small cheek. "Then it wouldn't be fair to him to make him hurt like that. He has done a lot for us. He got you new clothes and boots. He gave us a new home, food in our bellies, and a roof over our head. And we are together. So, to be fair, to be kind, I cannot let him hurt like I have."

Boden started to tear up. "So, I won't have a da anymore?"

Jordie started to tear up too as her son's heart fell. "That's right."

"Well, that's not fair to me!"

"Da has a good life here. People who love him, who care about him. I cannot take that away from him."

"I hate you!" Boden yelled. "I hate what you have done!"

Jordie started to cry for the first time ever in front of her son. "Well, my sweet Boden, I don't hate my choice to have you. I love you and you will always be my pride and greatest joy." She patted his leg, for he had rolled away in bed and turned his back on her. "Good night, babe. I love you."

Brokenhearted, Jordie went to the door and took a last look at her son.

"I love you, Boden," she said softly.

"I'm still mad at you."

"I know, sweetie, and that's all right, but I will always love you."

She never thought things would go this far. That people would be so unaccepting everywhere she happened to go. It was amazing to her how people were so biased, close-minded, so hurtful.

Even here, so far away from Veiled Hills.

CHAPTER TWENTY-FIVE

J ordie choked down sobs as she made her way up to their chamber. She got to the top and hung her head against the door. Her shoulders heaved as she cried. Once again, she was about to lose everything, but this time, she did it to herself. She did it to protect the man she loved.

Love?

Aye, she said to herself, *I do love him*.

Someone tapped her on the shoulder. She turned around, wiping at her eyes, and two men stared back at her.

"What do you want?" she asked angrily, recognizing the same men from earlier. *Throw me out like a burnt cake, indeed.*

"What spell have you put over our laird?" one of them demanded.

"What spell?" Jordie scowled. "Did you not hear me? I told him *not* to marry me."

"Then why did he?"

"How am I supposed to know?"

"Either you like him enough to divorce him and save him his title or there be someone else yer thinking of."

Jordie rolled her eyes, "Oh yeah, it's definitely someone else. In the seven years of living in solitude and being banished, had I a chance to meet someone other than a goat, cow, and a dog?"

"Woman, your mouth will run you into trouble."

"How can it? I haven't talked to anyone in seven years!"

"I dinnae ken what he sees in ye," the second man said, grumbling.

"You and me both," she said. "So, tell me, why are you here—unless it merely be to insult me?"

"We want ye ta sign that paper."

"And what makes you think I won't?"

"Me!" Locryn boomed.

●●●●●

He made his way up to their chamber, knowing that was where she would go. As he went up the stairs, he heard his friends' voices. They were trying to get her to follow through with the divorce, the Anormalis. He growled, angry that his friends would corner his wife. Then he heard her responses.

She was a beautiful mystery. She knew she deserved a better life but was willing to cast everything aside for him in a heartbeat. Her heart was just so giving and loving. How could anyone walk away from her? Why couldn't everyone see what he saw in her?

As for his best friends, he didn't think they would ever do something like this. They backed his wife into a corner, forcing her to sign a paper and end what he fought so hard to achieve. He had finally gained her trust, even though it ended with an ultimatum. Still, she liked him enough to trust him to a second chance. He knew his friends were looking out for him, but in truth, they were doing more damage than good.

After their fight in front of the whole clan, his sister Marcy pulled him in Thomas's study to talk sense into him, as did the rest of the family. Marcy wanted him to divorce Jordie. Even his mother was speechless; she had assumed that his wife would beg him to keep her. Bellamy even tried to get him to take the deal his mother made for him, but Locryn couldn't do it.

Then there was his brother and his wife, who told him not to listen to everyone. Thomas also told him that he would make sure he didn't lose his titles since he was laird and Locryn was the next in line.

He left in the middle of their scolding to go to his chamber, where he knew his wife would go. Now, here she was. Her back against the wooden door as his two friends had her cornered like a helpless rabbit.

She stared at him with shining eyes brimming with tears.

"Ye wilna divorce me, Jordie," he told her firmly.

Locryn shoved his friends aside and pulled his wife into his arms. He held her close to him, taking in the scent of her.

"Yer no' goin' ta do this."

She struggled against him, finally pulling away. "Aye, I will!"

"Dinna even think about it."

"And you want to hurt like I did? You want to lose everything you hold dear? What sane person would want that for themselves, for another, or for family?"

"Ye do things fer the person ye love."

Jordie looked at his blue eyes, unmoved and unbelieving. "You don't love me. You love the idea of me. You like me because I am different from all you have ever known."

Locryn put his hands on his hips. "I be no' goin' ta leave ye, Jordie. I made ye a promise."

Jordie looked at his friends, silently begging them for aid, but they only offered her harsh looks. "It is not your choice, Locryn. It is my choice. I must do what is right. Even though you promised, I don't hold you to it," she said and opened the chamber door.

He followed her inside, shutting the door behind him. Jordie undid the stays on her dress, stepping out of it quickly. She picked up her stained trews and tunic, putting them back on. She grabbed her bow and quiver, slinging it over her back, and cinched on her belt and hatchets.

Finally, Jordie grabbed the coat Locryn got her.

"Yer no' leavin'," he said, withholding her boots.

"I will leave with or without my boots, although I prefer to have them so these," she pointed to her slippers, "don't get ruined."

"Yer no' leavin', Jordie."

She came over to him, cupping his face in her hand. "Aye, I am," she said. She took the boots out of his hand and kissed him on the cheek.

On her way out, she faced Locryn's friends. "You are two honorable men who are loyal to your laird. Keep my son here, train him. He doesn't deserve to live out there alone."

They nodded.

"I will raise him with my boy," one said.

●●●●●

Jordie extended her hand in thanks. The man took it firmly by her forearm, sealing the deal. Locryn punched the stone wall in his fury, his knuckles cracking against the rock.

She looked at her husband for the last time. For days, she was so clouded by her distrust. But now she knew that Locryn was a sensitive man, attentive to the needs of the people around him. He was a kind man with a loving heart. And in order for her to give him the love he deserved, she had to leave.

But his friends stared at her like she had some sort of disease. They handed her the paper. Jordie cut her finger and signed it in blood. She didn't read it; she didn't care what it said. It was over and done with.

They were done.

Jordie turned around and went down the stairs, taking one last look at Locryn. He faced the wall, still as death. With a sigh, she headed down the stairs to her son's room.

Jordie opened the door, leaving it open in case Locryn tried to trap her inside.

She could feel a presence outside the door. When she looked, it was Locryn's friends and that beautiful lady from before—Locryn's sister-in-law, she remembered. Jordie inwardly groaned, but outwardly she nodded.

"Boden," Jordie spoke quietly, "I have something exciting I need to tell you."

She knew he wasn't sleeping at all. His eyes were closed too tightly. She stroked his face again and called his name. Boden opened his eyes, looking at her with a mixed expression.

"You are going to be trained among the men as a warrior," she told him, playing on his lifelong dreams.

"Really?" he asked, perking up.

"Aye," she said smiling, biting back the tears. "Da told me so a few moments ago."

She lied to her son for the first time in her life. Boden didn't need to know where she was going or that she was never returning. She left her trunk here, in hopes that someday, someone would give it to him, to remind Boden of who she was, what she smelled like. And when the men would retell Boden stories about her, she prayed they lied and made her sound better than she was.

Boden's smile split his face. "Thank you, Mum!" he said, hugging her neck.

"I love you," she said, kissing his cheek. "I love you very much!"

"I love you too, Mum."

"Get some sleep. You start training tomorrow."

Jordie brought the bow she had on her back around front. For the last seven years, she had a small ring on the top of the bow stave. It was the ring her mother had given her on her sixteenth birthday, the ring of her great-grandmother. She took it off her bow, twirling it in her fingers.

The ring had brought her luck. It was also the last item she had to leave behind. The beautiful lady entered the room, tears streaming down her cheeks. Jordie handed her the ring, closing her hand over top. Jordie knew the woman had the loving heart of a selfless mother. She was the only woman besides Hester to not judge her. The woman nodded to her, putting a soft hand on her arm.

"Jordie," the woman said, her voice as melodic as a fairy's, "I will look after him."

"Give that to him," Jordie whispered.

Then she turned back to her son, but he was already sleeping.

The woman was crying in sobs beside her. She was the only one who wasn't.

Jordie turned back to kiss his sleeping head again. "I love you so very much," she said, kissing his cheek. "Become the mightiest warrior Castre has ever seen," she whispered before walking away.

Jordie paused to glare at the man at the door. "You better keep your fucking promise to me," Jordie told him with a growl. "Train him to be the best warrior your clan has or will ever see."

The man grabbed the dagger from his belt and sliced his hand, offering it to her. Jordie took his dagger, doing the same. He grabbed her hand roughly, shaking it, making it an unbreakable pact. The man looked as coldly into her eyes as she did his.

"I do so swear to you, Jordie of Veiled Hills," he said, squeezing her hand, sealing the promise forever in blood.

"Thank you."

Jordie walked down the steps to her new future. She didn't look back. She couldn't. Things were set. Her son's future was protected. Everything she had ever desired for him was now secure.

People were lined up outside the West Tower. Lady Julia was at the bottom of the line of people. She stood tall and regal, glaring with hard eyes and pressed lips. Her emerald crown sat on top of her perfectly coifed, graying, hateful old head.

"Finally, the garbage be takin' itself oot," Julia said and spat at her feet.

Jordie smirked, "I like the sound you make when you shut up."

The former queen quaked with rage as she opened and shut her mouth like a dying fish gasping for air. "How dare ye insult me! I was just fixin' me son's mistake, like any good mother would do fer her child."

Jordie rolled her eyes. "If you want to know about mistakes, you should ask your parents."

Julia slapped her across the face. "How dare ye!"

Jordie smirked and Julia slapped her again.

"Dinna ever strike me wife again!" Locryn roared.

Jordie shoved her way past the nasty lady toward the castle gate, but Locryn caught her arm.

"Yer no' leavin', lass," he told her firmly, grabbing onto her arm. "And ye," he said to his mother, "be goin' ta treat me wife with respect."

"She be no' yer wife," the queen hissed. "I have the paper right here!"

Julia waved the parchment in her son's face like a battle flag. Locryn towered over his mother and snatched the paper right out of her hands and crumpled it in his fist.

"Jordie be me wife!" he said, "Ye will respect that." Locryn turned to his clan. "Ye all will!"

Still gripping Jordie's arm, he stalked back to the West Tower. Jordie didn't dare fight him. There was already enough tension going on between him and his mother.

Julia charged after them. "Ye will lose everythin'! I do so swear it!" she shrieked and started smacking her son.

Jordie broke free of his grasp and faced that old dragon of a mother-in-law. "You will *not* hit him," she said, grabbing the queen's hand, bending it backwards. "That is very unladylike behavior."

"Thomas be laird," Locryn said. "No' ye, Mother."

"Ye will regret this, Locryn," Julia said to their backs as they walked back up the tower steps.

CHAPTER TWENTY-SIX

Locryn dragged her back to their tower room and threw her inside. He locked the door behind him, scowling at her so fiercely. He was so intimidating. It was like he was begging for a fight, waiting to see if she would challenge him or not.

Which she wouldn't.

She might be stubborn but she wasn't dumb.

He strode over to the fire and shoved the piece of parchment into its center.

Then he walked over to her and took her small hands in his. "Dinna ever do somethin' like that again," he scolded, enveloping her in his arms.

"I just don't want you to lose everything," she said, hugging him back, burying her cold face in his chest.

Locryn kissed the top of her head. "So long as I have ye, I wilna lose anythin', love."

Jordie doubted that very much.

Julia was much like Jordie's sister Kathleen. They both desired everything to be done with propriety. Anything out of the social norm sent them reeling. Julia hated Jordie because of her colored past and therefore she would never allow her the time of day. Personality had no weight against past transgressions.

"I am going to check on Boden," she said, heading for the door.

Locryn grabbed her hand, lacing his thick calloused fingers in her small ones, following her.

Boden was sound asleep in his bed. Jordan was also on the bed, sleeping the other way. Sweet Ehlowen was asleep in the chair beside them both. It made her heart feel good that her son already had a best friend.

Trying not to wake them, Jordie went around the side to kiss her son on the head. The little man did not even move. Jordie smiled at him. Ehlowen opened her eyes briefly to glance at her. Jordie bent down to hug her fiercely then slid out of the room quietly.

Hand in hand, Jordie and Locryn went up the tower stairs to his room at the top. He opened the door for her and what they both found was astonishing. Jordie was surprised they both hadn't noticed it before now. Candles were lit in holders, wine and glasses were at the bedside table with a tray of breads, meats and cheeses, with a note:

Dearest Locryn and My Newest Sister,

Thank the Goddess you both are back. Just like I knew you would be. I cannot wait to get to know you, sister. Eat, drink, and be merry for tomorrow I am stealing you all day.

Love,

Ehlowen

Jordie blinked. "That was fast work."

Locryn nodded. "Aye."

Jordie smiled broadly, handing the note to her husband. "Is she always that thoughtful?"

Locryn read it, nodding his head. "Aye, she be a wonderful woman and ye will like her immensely."

"She seems quiet," Jordie remarked.

"She be no' quiet fer long, and since ye both be spendin' the day together tomorrow, she will talk more."

Jordie giggled softly.

He put the note down, coming over to her, caressing her lithe, toned shoulders with his strong calloused hands. He kissed her on the bottom of her collarbone, moving his lips up the side of her neck, ending on her cheek.

She shivered, closing her eyes at his light hot touch. She touched him back, wrapping her hands around his neck. Locryn slipped off her bow and her quiver, setting them down on the wooden floor. Jordie embraced him, clinging to his body, inhaling him deeply.

His hands went to her belt. It fell to the floor. Then they moved up her hips and towards her breasts as he removed her tunic.

"But ye, Jordie," he whispered huskily in her ear, "be the woman o' me dreams. Yer smart, cunnin', braw . . . and mine."

Did he really mean that? How could he? Jordie studied him, from the lines crossing his battle-worn face, to the firm set in his lips, to the color changing in his clear blue eyes that shone with desire.

She didn't mean to hurt him, to confuse him, to put him off like that. It had been years since anyone said anything remotely kind to her, calling her smart, brave—if that's what *braw* meant—and his. His own wife.

"You truly want me to be yours?" she asked.

Locryn's arms tightened around her. "Aye, ferever."

Their relationship was a tumultuous conundrum at best, but somehow, they drew closer together. They grew together. Locryn accepted her for who she was. He even embraced it. He knew that she was stubborn, a fierce mother, and a hunter, but those traits weren't flaws in his eyes. He only wanted her to give up some of that responsibility so he could take care of her. And she also accepted him for who he was—a mighty warrior, persistent and kind beyond reason. They were not perfect on their own but more perfect together.

"Ferever," he repeated, "because I love ye, Jordie."

She came closer to him, being bold, taking the initiative with a man for the first time. She placed her trembling fingers under his tunic and pulled it off his sculpted body. By the Goddess, he was incredible! His muscles glowed against the firelight; the scars across his body spoke of everything he had done to protect the ones he loved.

She got on her knees, kissing his stomach, moving and rising with her lips up to his chest, savoring the taste of his skin, the musky earth smell and the flavor of a man, of him, on her pink lips. Her hands roamed his body, getting acquainted with the touch and feel of him.

Locryn grabbed her, pulling her up towards him as she tried to make her way back down his stomach with her lips then pushed her down on the bed. He separated her legs with his knees, kissing her right underneath her breasts. His hot breath and gentle kisses caused her body to stir ferociously inside.

Jordie smiled and came close to his lips.

"And I love you," she said.

•••••

She let out a soft moan that would be the death of him, and by the holy Goddess, she was so beautiful. Her long dark red hair cascaded over the bed like a river. Her stomach was tight, smooth. The black leather trews she wore hugged her slim body so perfectly, it was absolutely tantalizing. His fingers itched to remove them.

He moved his calloused hands against her soft stomach to her back, working her trews off her body. She wriggled with him, allowing him access to the part of her that she had guarded for over seven years. Her eyes were glazed over, glossy with lust and the want, the need, to be loved.

She wriggled underneath him some more, trying to kick off the boots that were still on her feet. Locryn bent down on the floor, helping her get her boots off. He kissed the tops of her feet, going up both legs with kisses but just stopping outside her womanly center.

Jordie sighed.

An idea formed in his mind.

Locryn got off the bed, leaving his half-naked woman waiting for him. He grabbed a blanket that was over the back of a chair and laid it down beside the fire. Then he snatched the pillows off the bed, putting them on his makeshift bed by the fire.

Jordie walked over to him, kicking off her black trews as she went. She boldly pushed him down on the blanket, straddling him like a horse she had long wished to ride. Her lips lightly brushed his at first, teasing him.

Growling, he turned her over. It was her turn to surrender that part of her. For years, she had done everything in her power to thrive, to succeed in a world where she was not wanted. Now that wasn't the case anymore. He was going to succeed in life for her, so she could thrive in a different way.

Instinctively she moved her legs apart, allowing him entry to her sweet core. He touched her inner thigh, moving his hands towards her domain. She bucked at his touch, letting him know that she was ready for him.

Her hands moved towards his trews quickly, removing them with her nimble fingers. "I need you," she whispered.

"What be the hurry, Jordie?" he asked, just to hear her answer.

She looked at him thoughtfully. "What if this all is just some sort of dream, and when it's over, I am alone again?"

"Me sweet wife," he whispered, "I promise ye, I be no' leavin' and this be no' a dream."

She slipped her hands behind his neck. "I love you, Locryn."

He glided on top of her, positioning himself to enter her, "And I love ye, stubborn woman," he teased, nibbling her neck.

She bucked beneath him as he entered her warm, wet center, sliding in and out. Jordie moaned under him, moving with him, coming in such a short time. He loved the sounds she made, the way she glowed in the firelight, how her skin blazed bronze, glimmering in sweat. How her hair fell over the blanket, wavy and flowing like water.

She wreathed underneath him, her hands going from his back to his arms, feeling him, touching him. Her hands roamed his stomach going lower to where she reached for his manhood as he entered her over and over.

He never thought coupling with a woman like her would be enjoyable. Her feisty, tenacious side was hard to handle at times. But it all made up who this woman was. And he loved every little part of her.

This beautiful strong woman was his, now and forever. He would never let her go. He was going to cherish her in this moment and every moment after. He drove into her, filling her small body with his seed. As he filled her, he looked long into her eyes, knowing that their children would be a part of her.

"I love you, Locryn," she breathed huskily as he satisfied her yet another time.

He kissed her ardently. "And I love ye, Jordie."

Locryn rolled off of her, making her scoot closer to the fire so she could stay warm. He leaned up on his elbow, looking at his wife, her body covered in a thin sheen of sweat.

"Satisfied?" he asked chuckling.

Jordie rolled over to face him. "Aye, thank you," she replied, kissing the inside of his hand.

"Be ye ready fer tomorrow?"

"As long as I don't have to wear a dress," she smirked.

"Will ye please wear one fer me?"

"That depends, husband."

Locryn snorted. "Depends on what?"

"Depends on how long you plan on loving me for."

He smiled at her as he caressed her hair, rolling on top of her, stroking her sweet body with his fingers. "Ferever, wife," he kissed her. "Ferever," he said as he plunged into her again for the second time that night.

CHAPTER TWENTY-SEVEN

He was finally asleep, snoring into a pillow. A small puddle of drool escaped his mouth. She brushed his tangled hair out of his face, kissing him for the last time on his cheek.

Jordie silently pulled on her stained tunic and trews, watching the man she loved sleep. She tiptoed to the other side of the bed and gathered her boots, coat, belt, bow and quiver.

Silently, she opened the chamber door and left.

She let out the breath she was holding.

Sitting on the step, she pulled on her boots, lacing them up to the middle of her calf. She slung the quiver and bow on her back and headed down the West Tower stairs.

Jordie paused in front of Boden's door and peeked in. Ehlowen was asleep in a chair next to the hearth with her babe on her chest. Boden was still sound asleep, covers thrown off his body. Merle slept by Boden's head.

As soundlessly as she could, she walked over to her son, kissing him on the cheek.

"I love you, my sweet boy," she whispered.

Tears stung her eyes as she walked away for the final time.

Night never seemed so long and so lonely as it did then. The moon was still out and the cold nipped sharply. Torches glowed around her, giving off the faintest amount of light.

Snow started to fall around her.

She smiled at the crystalline cold kisses that fell on her head. Snow would absorb her sound and mask her trail as she made her way out of Drensent. She walked towards the castle gate which was guarded by two men. Jordie lied and told them she was going hunting, so they raised the portcullis for her.

With a final look back, she walked out of Drensent, this time for good, heading down the road she traveled the day before. Jordie shifted the weight of her bow and quiver as she walked.

"You're making a mistake," a familiar voice said to her.

Jordie looked off to her left, seeing a gray hound dog jog up to her.

"Good morning, Aramoren," she said.

"It's not morning, my dear," he corrected.

Jordie looked at the fading darkness giving way to a cloud morning. "Morning enough."

"Not satisfied with last night's tumbles?"

Jordie walked around him, snorting derisively, heading on down the roadway. "Perfectly satisfied, if you must know, but that is not the reason I am leaving."

"Ah, playing the martyr then, are we?"

"It is the right thing to do," she said. "We aren't married anymore. Even if he did burn the paper, his mother and his clan witnessed it."

Aramoren trotted in dog form beside her. "You humans are so interesting," he chortled, "I missed your annoying quirks."

Jordie shot him an icy glare. "I missed it when I thought you were just a hound."

Hurt, Aramoren sniffed, "Turn around."

Then he galloped off into the woods.

Jordie stopped in her tracks and sighed. She was at the top of the hill that she came up yesterday. The place she thought was going to be her confining prison turned out to be the place where she left her heart.

"I love you enough to do what is right," she said and walked down the road alone.

•••••

Locryn woke with a start. A sensation in his gut told him that something was wrong. Hazily he reached out for his wife, but she wasn't there. He sat up, still naked from the night before. He looked around the room for his wife, but she wasn't there.

He got up and dressed, looking around for any sign that she was gone.

Her bow and quiver were gone.

Her clothes, boots, coat, and belt were all gone.

Locryn pulled his boots on, grabbed his sword, slung it on his back, and bounded down the castle stairs two at a time. He stopped at Boden's door, trying to keep the noise to a minimum. He peeked inside, scanning the room for Jordie but she wasn't there either.

Ehlowen was awake, nursing Katell. Locryn motioned for his sister-in-law to come over.

"What's the matter?" she asked, hushed but concerned.

"Jordie's missin'."

Ehlowen gasped. "Already? It's snowing, Locryn!"

He cursed under his breath and dashed down the stairs. Once he reached the landing, he ran to the stables. He opened the door himself and shoved the stablemaster out of the way to get to his horse.

He waited long enough to throw a bridle on the stallion before mounting. He kicked the beast into a gallop, bursting out the stable doors and into the morning light. He went straight for the iron gate that was closed.

"Raise it up," he shouted.

"Ho, Locryn," Gordon yelled. "What's the hurry?"

Locryn dismounted and grasped Gordon by the collar of his tunic. "Where be me wife?" he roared.

"I don't know," Gordon said, shoving him off. "Blake and Rory said she left this morning to go hunting."

Locryn mounted his horse. "She lied."

"How do you know she lied? She is a hunter."

"Because she lied," Aramoren said at the gate, "for the second and last time ever."

Swords swished out of their sheaths as Locryn yelled for his men to hold. He glared at the shifter. What did the dog man know that he did not? With every breath he took, Jordie was getting farther away from him. He had to get her back.

Aramoren grinned with his large, pointed teeth. "We meet again."

"Where be me wife?" Locryn growled.

"Out there, in the snow. Wandering, the little martyr."

"Martyr?"

Aramoren rolled his yellow eyes. "By her own hand this time, I assure you."

"She left to save Locryn," Gordon surmised.

"Now, you get it," Aramoren laughed. "I like him."

Locryn commanded the men at the gate to open for him, which they did so hurriedly. Gordon motioned for a few other men to follow.

"She's not far," Aramoren said, licking his paw. "She can't go forward because she keeps looking back."

Gordon waved for men to follow him to the stables. Locryn waited impatiently for them to hurry back. It didn't take long but every second felt like hours, and all of it together felt like a lifetime.

Jordie was on foot. She wouldn't want to be tracked down or found. She would take to the main road because she was unfamiliar with the forest. That was where he would head first.

The iron gates rose, and the sun glowed bright against his back. The snow stopped. The morning animals were quiet.

With a shout, Locryn called his men behind him and off they rode.

•••••

Every few minutes she would check over her shoulder to see if anything or anyone followed her. The forest was silent, like that of a grave. The only sound she heard was the crunching of snow under her boots.

Jordie trudged along the road for a while before veering west. She didn't want to head back south on her family's land. Nor did she want to go east to the place from where beings like Aramoren hailed. North was impossible; she would waste time trying to go around the mountain range. Going west was her best bet at finding a new life.

She tried her best to not think about Boden or Locryn. But that was impossible. She missed them both, and with each step, she tried to be braver and continue. Jordie wiped at her eyes.

Something pickled at the back of her neck. It wasn't the cold.

258

Jordie took to the nearest tree, climbing the low branches, and waited.

JORDIE IN CHARGE

CHAPTER TWENTY-EIGHT

Her tracks were still fresh in the light dusting of snow. Aramoren was nowhere to be seen which suited him just fine. Gordon and Finn rode beside him and about ten of their most sharp-sighted men followed.

Locryn trotted down the road, calling her name, but all that answered was a slight breeze. The clouds above hung dark and low. Waiting. The trees were silent; the whole forest of Drensent was eerily soundless.

He trotted until her tracks became barely noticeable before he stopped. He twirled his horse in a circle, scanning the tops of the branches, knowing Jordie was intelligent enough to be in them.

Stubborn, sneaky woman, he thought, *where be ye?*

A howl sounded off in the distance.

Locryn looked to the west.

"That's wapako," Gordon said.

Finn and Gordon looked at each other, their faces strained in worry.

"Ye dinna think . . ." Finn trailed off.

Locryn spurred his horse towards the sound. He let go of the reins, unsheathing his sword. A pack of wapako ran madly in circles around something bleeding on the ground.

Locryn's heart jumped in his throat.

"No!" he screamed as he began slicing and slashing through the deformed beasts.

The animals looked like twisted combinations of wolf, bear, and wolverine. Thick fur added to their bulk although they were tall and lanky like wolves. Their snouts were short like a bear's, with bear-like ears, but their fur matched more the pattering of the wolverine.

Locryn got to the fallen carcass. It was a holleristo deer, not Jordie. Relief flooded him. She was still alive—but out there somewhere.

Howls erupted from the forest around him. Out of the shadows, the wapako ran. They kept coming, dozens of beasts, leaping from behind boulders and bushes. Two of his men succumbed to their claws. A wapako launched itself at Gordon, knocking the burly man off his horse.

Locryn raced to him, fighting to pull the animal off, when something came whizzing into its neck.

●●●●●

Deep howls echoed through the forest around her, getting closer. Her heart stopped. Then came the tramp of paws. They passed under her tree, sniffing and drooling, and surrounded the base of her tree.

Jordie licked her lips.

Quietly, she climbed higher into the tops. Then she leaned over, trying to make her way to the next tree that could support her weight. But her attempt was folly. The beasts, whatever they were, followed her from one tree to the next.

Jordie's breath caught in her throat. The beasts were leaping at her, snapping their ravenous jaws. She could hear the clashing of their teeth, like vases smashing on walls. Her heart beat wildly as she picked her way through the treetops.

Then one of them howled.

The group below her took off, loping towards the clearing ahead of her.

Jordie lowered herself down the tree, hearing the pounding of horse hooves in the distance.

Locryn, she thought with a smile. *Locryn!*

Without a moment's hesitation, she dropped to the ground, running towards the sounds of horses whinnying and snarling jaws snapping. Jordie ran as fast as she could, drawing her bow and nocking an arrow.

She came out of the trees, bursting out of the bushes. Instinctually, she scrambled up to higher ground. The sickening beasts attacked the Drensent men as she climbed a nearby rock. She scanned the battle frantically, looking for Locryn.

Jordie saw him, trying to pull a monstrous animal off Gordon. She nocked her arrow, taking careful aim. Its claws

263

dug into his flesh. Gordon screamed. She released her arrow, getting the creature in the neck.

She looked around her, taking down any giant, rabid beasts that the men were fighting. Arrow after arrow she sent flying through the air until she reached in her quiver and snatched only air. Jordie jumped down off her rock, running towards the fray.

She ran towards Finn who had a beast trying to corner him against two others. Jordie threw her hatchet at the animal, clipping it in the shoulder. She stopped to grab an arrow out of one of the fallen, taking careful aim and getting it in the mouth as it tried to bite Finn.

Soon Locryn's men gained the upper hand against the wild animals, sending them all loping away. After she retrieved her hatchet, she looked at the men who remained. Her former husband came striding toward her, scowling. Jordie backed away but tripped over one of the dead animals, falling backwards on her buttocks in the snow.

He leaned down and picked her up by her tunic collar.

"What the fuck were ye thinkin', Jordie?" he seethed.

Jordie's chin wobbled. "I—" she licked her lips "—I didn't want your mother to make your life miserable."

Locryn set her down. "I love ye, Jordie, and we be married. And curse me mum, she wilna make me miserable."

Jordie shook her head. "I signed the paper and your mother saw it, as did the clan," she reminded him. "We're not married."

"We be married."

"Wow, this is quite the mess, Jordie! But may I say—fine shooting," Aramoren stated, coming out of the wood.

Locryn groaned.

"Hello, Aramoren," Jordie greeted.

Aramoren linked his hairy arms around both her and Locryn, looking from one to the other. "Trust," he said. "Didn't I tell you both to trust each other?"

Jordie smirked, but Locryn wasn't as amused.

The shifter had been right all along. Aramoren meant for her to entrust her heart to a man who would love her unconditionally, a man who would protect her and honor her. Stupidly, she didn't listen, even after she discovered last night that Locryn was her heart.

But Aramoren also meant for her to trust in the Goddess, that Corwaithe's plan for her was so much more than what she ever thought it could be. That the obstacles Corwaithe put in front of her were only temporary. That Jordie needed to trust and have faith in Corwaithe that she would make everything better after a few trials of personal growth.

The shifter sighed. "Well, now that you both have *finally* figured it out, I'm going home."

"Until we meet again," Jordie said and waved him off.

"Nope," the dog man said and bounded off.

Gordon came over to her, holding his injured arm. Jordie stood, gazing at all the men who were looking at her.

265

Jordie licked her lips nervously. Finn stared at her as did the other eight men who were still standing.

"Is," she began, then cleared her throat, "everyone all right?"

Finn nodded. "Aye," he responded, leaning heavily on his sword. "Ye all right, Jordie?"

"Yeah," she replied a little shakily. "What are these things?" she asked, kicking the dead carcass of one nearby.

"Wapako," Gordon replied. "Ye saved us all, lass."

Jordie snorted, shaking her head. "I did not."

Locryn took her hand, spinning her towards him. "Aye, ye did, ye stubborn braw woman," he said and kissed her on the lips.

"You're not mad at me?"

"Nay," he said and pulled her into a hug. "I ken why ye did it, love. I just didna want ta lose ye. I love ye, Jordie."

"I love you too," she said, burying her cold face into his warm body. "What about your mother?"

Locryn shrugged. "What about her?"

"Are you not worried she will do something?"

"Nay," he said, kissing her forehead. "If I was concerned, ye would ken, all right?"

Jordie grinned. "Let's go home."

"Finally," Finn said. "I thought I was goin' ta bleed oot."

"Oh," Jordie said, "let's stay here so you can finish then."

"Yer trouble," Finn said with a smile, "but I be glad yer apart o' this clan."

"Aye," Gordon seconded.

The rest of the men cheered. Jordie smiled, feeling a sense of comradery, she had never experienced before. Locryn mounted his horse, offering her his hand.

"Let's go home, wife," he said with a smile.

Jordie looked behind her at the scene of all of those dead animals. She looked long at each one with an arrow in its body. Each one she took down to save the men who came looking for her.

She smiled faintly, looking back at Locryn. "With you, I'll go anywhere."

JORDIE IN CHARGE

CHAPTER TWENTY-NINE

I t was mid-morning when they came back through the iron gates of Drensent. Thankfully, people were going about their daily tasks and didn't give her a second glance. Locryn dismounted, helping her down next, then motioning for someone to take his horse.

He took her up to the West Tower for her to change out of her bloody clothes. He too was covered in gore from the battle with the wapako. Jordie tiredly trudged up the stairs, her feet scuffing against the stone.

Locryn opened the door for her and she entered, immediately shucking her clothing. They were beyond repair. Jordie threw her tunic in the fire. She took off her trews, looking them over for holes or any sign of damage. Her trews were still good.

She turned her back to Locryn, warming up by the fire. Jordie closed her eyes, savoring the heat against her skin.

Locryn came up behind her, lightly brushing her arms with his fingertips, "I can warm ye up faster," he said, kissing her neck.

Her head fell back against his chest, his lips roaming up to the side of her neck by her ear.

"I'm sure you could, but you can't put food in my belly," she said as her stomach rumbled.

"I can fill it," he teased.

Jordie turned around, casting him doleful eyes. "I'm hungry," she said, whining like a spoiled child.

Locryn smiled, kissing her on her lips. "Let's get ye fed then."

Jordie washed the blood from her hands and face quickly. She put on the same dress she wore last night and swept up her tangled locks into a knot at the back of her head.

Locryn draped her coat over her shoulders, took her arm, and led her out the door. Boden came bounding up to the stairs, clueless as to where she had been or what happened.

Thank the Goddess he doesn't know, she thought.

Snow lightly sparkled the ground. Gleaming, frosty iciness crunched beneath her feet as she walked with her family to the dining hall. Jordie relished the crisp air and clear blue sky. Thankfully, the clouds had cleared, which meant no snow and only a bright sunny day ahead.

Boden ran off to look for Jordan and his grandmother Hester, who was also one of her very first and newest of friends as well. Jordie couldn't keep the smile from her face. Everyone around her was walking past her smiling, joyful. The happiness was palpable and wonderfully contagious.

Jordie entered into the dining hall through the enormous oaken doors. They were thicker and wider than her hands breadth. The cold stone floor was swept and a couple of lads laid out the rush mats.

Locryn's mother was already at the head of the table, glowering at her as she straightened her back and posed regally. To her amazement, Laird Thomas and Queen Ehlowen moved to the table below Julia. Locryn pulled out a seat for Jordie and she sat down beside her husband.

"Good morning, Ehlowen," Jordie said, sitting down across from her. "Good morning, Thomas," she said, nodding to her brother-in-law.

Ehlowen smiled brightly. "Good morning, Jordie. Are you ready for our day?"

Jordie had forgotten all about the note her sister-in-law left for her. She wondered what Ehlowen had planned, but at the same time, she dreaded to find out. More than likely, it had to do with dresses and seamstresses. Which meant lace, matching slippers, and heavy jewelry were also involved. Jordie wanted to groan but refrained out of respect.

"What will we be doing?" Jordie asked.

Ehlowen laughed. "We are going to broaden your wardrobe, dear sister!"

Julia's chair screeched out on the stone floor. "Dinna waste yer time, Ehlowen," she chastised. "Ye canna put a dress on a pig."

Jordie ignored her. "Thank you," Jordie told Ehlowen, looking pleadingly at her husband who was busy smirking at her from behind a roll.

"Do you not like dresses, Jordie?" Ehlowen asked.

"Other than this, I haven't worn one in a long time."

Ehlowen placed a hand on hers. "Well, we will start with just one dress then. If you don't like it, we can make you some new trews and tunics. Sound fair enough to try?"

"Ehlowen," Julia commanded, "dinna waste the coin. She be leavin' soon—the nerve o' that whore!"

Thomas rose from the table, leaning close to his mother. "Enough. Jordie be a part o' this family," he said with finality, "and ye *will* accept that."

"Mother," Locryn added, "I have tried ta let yer intolerance slide, but I wilna no longer. If ye canna be nice ta me wife, then yer no' me mother."

Julia turned pale, walking away from the table.

The two men sat down, rejoining the women's conversation as if nothing happened. Jordie looked at her husband, brows furrowed, wondering if he happened to be all right.

"Are you ready to try, Jordie?" Ehlowen asked again.

Jordie looked at Ehlowen tentatively but nodded. "I am."

"Wonderful," Ehlowen said clapping her hands together. "Eat up, because after that, we have to plan tonight's feast."

"Another one?"

"Why of course! We are celebrating you being a part of this clan."

"Oh," Jordie said surprised, blinking rapidly. "Thank you."

After that, Jordie tucked into her breakfast. It was a light morning meal of sweetmeats, porridge, and dried fruit, but it was all so delicious. She had three bowls before she was finally done. Locryn stared wide-eyed at her progress as Thomas remarked at how much she put away.

"I was hungry," Jordie said after she spooned the last bite into her mouth.

"I could tell," Thomas chuckled. "Eat more, lass, if ye be hungry."

"I am full now," she replied sipping some watered wine.

Julia came to their table, ignoring Jordie. "Locryn, me son, I told ye ta divorce this woman and no' let her come back. Why canna ye be an obedient man and listen ta yer wise mum?" Julia said, placing a maternal hand on her son.

Locryn shrugged his mother off, glaring.

Julia came around to her, lifting her braid up and inspecting the ends, grumbling. Jordie placed her palms face down on the table, her eyes shooting daggers at the wall. Locryn placed his hand on her knee.

"Mother," Thomas said, rising in his chair. "Enough. Jordie be Locryn's wife. Stop treatin' her this way."

Julia swung Jordie's braid. "I will speak how I please, Thomas, and I will do as I please."

"Then yer no' me mother," Locryn growled.

"Then please take your drama elsewhere," Jordie said. "And please don't touch me."

"How dare ye speak ta me mother, yer lady queen, in that manner!" shrieked a woman Jordie had yet to meet. "She be above ye, ye bloody whore!"

Jordie laughed, rising out of her chair. "Nay, we are all equals under Corwaithe, but if you wish to nit-pick, I am a princess of Drensent, as I am married to Laird Locryn."

The woman got up real close to Jordie, mere inches away from her face, her red pudgy face scowling.

"Marcy," Thomas called, "dinna get involved or ye will be in trouble."

Marcy turned to her brother. "I will do as I please," she barked at him. "And ye," she glared at Jordie, "yer day o' reckonin' be comin!"

"Brilliant," Jordie replied, edging closer. "I cannot wait for the invitation."

Thomas strode around the table and pointed to the door. "Yer done!" he seethed. "And ye mother, yer done as well."

Julia tried to interject but Thomas held up his hands. "I be Laird, since ye both have fergotten. And I be done with ye both. Yer no' ta come oot o' yer chambers if ye canna be nice. Now go, because I be damned done."

Locryn snorted.

Julia stormed off with Marcy at her heels. Jordie sat back down, shaking her head. She began chomping on another sweetmeat when the grinning face of Thomas caught her eye. Jordie looked up to see him slowly start breaking down into a fit of laughter.

Confused, Jordie asked, "Something funny, my king?"

Thomas slowly sobered. "*I canna wait fer the invitation?* Och, that was funny."

Jordie smiled.

"Mum has changed since the death o' our father, Conner. She be no' who she used ta be. But cheers ta ye fer standin' up fer yerself."

Jordie nodded. "I am just tired of being condemned as something that I'm not. I'm not a bad person."

Thomas nodded then smiled, taking her hand in his and squeezing it. "Aye, Jordie, ye be no'. Welcome ta the family," he told her, getting up out of his seat and kissing her on the cheek. "Now I be stealin' yer husband ta go take care o' some things. Ye lassies be all right fer a wee bit? And Jordie, we be family, so no titles, all right?"

Ehlowen nodded. "Aye, husband. Be safe."

Thomas kissed her soundly. "Yes, wife."

Locryn came up to her, smiling kindly at her. "Ye'll have a battle on yer hands now with Marcy."

"I know."

"Aye, I be sure ye can handle it," he said, kissing her zealously on the lips. "I love ye. I will be back soon."

"I love you too."

"I be takin' our son with me. He needs ta watch and learn."

"All right. See you before dark?"

"Aye, wife."

Ehlowen came up beside her, linking their arms together. "Now that the men are gone, let's go into the kitchens to plan for the feast. Then off to my tower room to make you a dress."

Jordie wrinkled her nose. "Is 'dress' singular or plural?"

"How many dresses do you own?"

"One."

"Then plural."

Jordie looked at the ground and smiled. Indeed, her wardrobe was going to broaden.

CHAPTER THIRTY

The feasting meal was planned in no time. The cook was going to use the leftover broeshilak and turn it into stew. Ehlowen asked for Tosh and a few men to bring down two red holleristo deer. Jordie so wished to join the hunt, but she knew Ehlowen would be upset.

After the meals were planned, Ehlowen led her back to her chambers in the South Tower. North Tower was in front of West Tower, the one she and Locryn shared. East Tower was across from North Tower and finally South Tower South was across from West, Ehlowen explained. She promised Jordie a full tour of the grounds after they made her dress.

Jordie didn't know how this woman planned to make a dress in such a short amount of time, unless she meant to use magic or had one in store. But her sister-in-law was full of surprises. When they entered the first room in the South Tower, inside were four ladies. Two were laying out fabric and patterns while the other two were already sewing pieces together.

Jordie hesitated at the threshold, but the women smiled back and greeted her kindly and praised her marksmanship and bravery. Jordie thanked them all before inspecting the fabric laid out before her. All of this she could choose from, and the seamstresses would use it to make whatever she desired. There were cotton, wool, and silk in a rainbow of colors. Some bolts had patterns of flowers, some with a swirling paisley print, others with stripes and crisscrossed patterns. With all of this fabric, she could make bundles of tunics and trews.

She reached out to touch the silks.

"Pick whatever you like, Jordie," Ehlowen encouraged.

Jordie shook her head. "I don't even know!"

"Well, try something on first to see if you like the color and the fit."

"This should be your size, my lady," a woman came up, handing her a dress. "If not, then we will measure you and start again."

"Oh, marvelous color and style, Willa!" Ehlowen remarked while escorting Jordie to a changing curtain, knowing Jordie didn't want to be touched.

Jordie reluctantly took off the dress Locryn got her and her blue leather slippers to put on this dress that Ehlowen so wanted for her to wear. Ehlowen then passed her a soft shift to wear underneath the dress. It wasn't at all bad looking. It was well made and thankfully without frilly lace. She liked how plain it was. The dress had a decorative tie on the bodice like the ties on her boots, which she rather liked. Plus, it was her favorite color, dark green, with rich cream-colored embroidered accents around the collar and hems on the arms and bottom of the dress.

Jordie came out from behind the changing curtain.

278

Ehlowen clapped her hands. "Oh, Jordie—it fits you so well!"

Jordie spun in a circle, feeling the skirts swish against her hips. "It's surprisingly warm."

"Warmer than your hunting trews and tunic?"

Jordie nodded. "Those trews are made out of a broeshilak. The leather is thinner than most, but it's warm in winter and not too hot in summer. It's durable like the tiny creatures are, so I wear them."

"Will you be wearing a dress from now on?" Ehlowen asked, smiling.

"I am not going to go hunting in a dress, but I will wear one when I'm not." Jordie spun in a circle again. "They're not as bad as I remembered," she giggled.

The ladies laughed with her. She spent the next hour or so picking out fabric not only for a new pair of hunting clothes, but for a few new dresses as well. She selected matching slippers to wear around the castle. The kindness around her made her heart want to explode.

"Thank ye, Jordie," Willa said, embracing her.

Jordie awkwardly hugged her back. "For what?" she asked, confused.

"Ye saved me husband today against the wapako."

Jordie smiled, "Ah—then Finn is your husband? Well, he is my clansman, and that is what we do."

Then the women wanted to hear the whole story from Jordie. So, she took a seat and explained why she left. She told them about how the large beasts found her tree and then went after the men.

"Were they scary?" Willa asked, clutching her skirts.

Jordie nodded. "Unlike anything I have ever seen."

"Me Gordon said ye were a brave lass," Vorrie said, sewing the sleeve of a dress. "Thank ye, Jordie."

Jordie nodded, uncomfortable with the topic. The ladies continued to discuss her while she sat there, shifting in her seat. Jordie didn't care for being discussed or praised. She only jumped into the action because it was the right thing to do. She didn't expect anything out of it.

"So," Ehlowen said, nudging her arm, "care to play a board game with me?"

Jordie smiled at her sister-in-law, nodding, while Ehlowen brought over the game. Ehlowen sat with her babe in one arm as they played this game of concentration and wits, a game that Ehlowen called chess. It took her some time to figure out the rules, but once she did, she had fun.

Ehlowen called for refreshments, which Jordie went to get up to get, but Ehlowen pulled her back down, smiling. It had been years since she'd had servants to care for her needs. This was going to take some getting used to.

"Are you all right, Jordie?" Ehlowen asked after a while.

"Aye," Jordie nodded, getting out of her chair, "I just need some air."

Jordie embraced her sister-in-law and left the South Tower. She needed to walk and get some fresh air. Was she really ready to be treated like a princess again?

CHAPTER THIRTY-ONE

Jordie walked around the castle grounds by herself, nodding to the people she passed. As she looked for her son, she suddenly remembered that Locryn took him that morning. So now Jordie had two menfolk to find.

Jordie walked around the castle grounds twice, going up on the wall walks and searching everywhere. She went inside the castle keep to the king's study from the night before, but they weren't there. She came back outside to the bright afternoon light and found her son. The clan children, including her son, were out in the middle of the small clearing near the castle wall, trying their best to shoot a bow.

This will be fun, she thought to herself as she approached the kids. *I can teach them how to shoot a bow properly.*

"Gah, I canna make it work," one boy said.

"Let me try next, Homer," said Jordan.

Homer handed the bow over to Jordan, who nocked an arrow and at least hit their makeshift target. It was a bundle of hay with a cloth over top and painted marks on the cloth.

She watched them all making rounds between each other, each one trying to make the arrow go.

When it was Jordan's turn again, he struck the hay near the same spot as last time. Jordie complimented him on hitting the target but suggested he raise his elbow to make his aim true.

"Can ye teach us, milady?" Homer asked.

"Aye, but I will tell you a secret first," she whispered to the gathering children. "*Call me Jordie.*"

The kids laughed.

"Now," she began, "is this one bow all you have?"

"Nay, Jordie," a little girl said. "There be more at the arsenal."

"Take me there and let's see if we can get you all a bow to start practicing with," she told the little girl with a smile.

"Truly? I can learn?" she asked.

"Aye," she told them all, "it's very important that you all know how to defend yourself, man or woman. And it's also important to learn how to hunt in case you are ever separated from the clan."

Together they raced off to the arsenal, making all sorts of clamor. The man came out, looking at her with perked brows of curiosity, as the children all begged for bows and arrows. Jordie nodded her consent as the weapons master gave them a small bow and a quiver. He followed them back to the wall where they practiced, watching intently as Jordie gathered the children around her.

She smiled at them all. "Now, for a first lesson," she said, "who here can tell me the parts of a bow?"

One little boy raised his hand. "Me! I'm Nort, milady."

"Hello, Nort. Can you tell me the parts of a bow?"

"Fletching," he said proudly.

"That is part of the arrow, my dear," she said and proceeded to explain all the parts of the bow. "Now, today you will work on how to correctly hold the handle, use the sight, nock your arrow, and pull the bow."

She used Boden's bow as an example and demonstrated each step. Jordie drew a line in the ground fifteen paces from the target, an adequate distance from the target for the small children.

"Now, put your right foot here, Nort, on this line. Keep it straight. Take your left foot and put it slightly out, here," she told him, kicking his feet into position. "Now nock your arrow," she said, coming up behind him and helping him do so with the arrow pointed down at the dirt. "Keep your arrow down, children, so no one gets shot."

Nort nocked his arrow. "Like this?" he asked.

"Perfect. Now straighten your back, and pull your butt under yourself."

The kids all laughed and so did she.

"Now, draw back and tell me what you see when you look down the shaft of the arrow."

"I see the target."

"All right, now focus on which part you want to shoot at—use your eyes, they will guide your hand."

Nort stood there, arrow nocked, draw pulled back to his ear. Finally, he let out his breath like she told him, releasing the arrow. He hit the target on the second color towards the very center. Jordie praised him well. Nort jumped around, happy that he did it right, and ending his capers with a hug to Jordie's leg.

The weapons master brought over small vambraces for the children. Jordie thanked him and together they fitted each child with a vambrace for their bow-holding arm. The children couldn't be more excited, talking animatedly about all the new things they were getting to practice with.

Once Nort was done, she taught all eight kids, including her son, how to shoot properly. Then she and Weapons Master Jower explained how to use, care for, and store the weapons properly.

Little Mella was exceptionally good. Jordie was pleased with how quickly she caught on to everything. All her students were doing well. Nort was more of a powerhouse archer; his little body was strong and he managed a good pull on the arrow. Mella, Boden, Kurt, and Jordan were more accurate shooters, and their strength would come with time. Brisa, Callie, and Pollo were still trying their best to get their stance perfected. They were intellectual learners who had to observe, then do.

"They be doin verra well, milady," Jower commented.

"Jordie," Jordie smiled at him. "And I have good students. But do you think I should have asked their parents first?"

284

"Their parents wilna mind much," he said with a wink. "Yer certainly makin' yer mark in this clan."

"I only wish to be accepted as an equal. I don't want the special treatment just because Laird Locryn is my husband."

Jower chuckled. "Good, because I be tired o' bein' polite," he said, clapping her on the shoulder. "Their families wilna care. We be a pretty laid-back clan, Jordie."

"Aye, Jordan always wanted to learn how to shoot," Hester said approaching them all. "You got the clan talking, yet again."

Jordie rolled her amber eyes. "I'm sure I do."

Hester and Jower laughed. Jordie walked over to the children, telling them that the lesson was over for today, but they could practice more after the nooning meal tomorrow. With sad grumbles, the kids took their bows and equipment back to the arsenal, putting them back where they got them.

Jordie looked at the sky, judging the clouds and the sunset to come. She told her friends that it was going to rain soon, but instead it started sprinkling right then. Jordie grumbled. She didn't like being wet.

"You best get ready for the feast anyway," Hester told her. "Locryn said that he cannot wait to see you in a dress."

"Then he should have come outside because I am wearing one right now."

"But this is a special feast, Jordie. You're a part of the clan now."

"But I don't need a feast to honor that."

285

Hester put her hands on her hips. "You're so stubborn."

Jordie laughed, "Just remember, Locryn brought me here."

"Go get cleaned up," Jower said smiling broadly. "I heard the feast be a special one this eve."

Jordie smiled at them both. "I'm just going for the food."

"There will be plenty of that," Hester replied.

"Aye, and you can eat happily in your new gown as well," Ehlowen came over to tell her.

"New gown?"

"We made it for you while you were instructing," she said, taking Jordie's arm. "Shall we?"

Jordie couldn't tell the queen no, especially after all Ehlowen had done for her over the course of the day. Together, the two friends walked back to Jordie's chamber, and Hester followed. Jordie looked all over for her husband but he was naught to be seen.

The doubts crept in. Where had he been all day? Could he not stand to be around her? Had he changed his mind about her?

Jordie climbed the stairs to the top chamber. The two cushioned chairs were moved out of the way to make room for a copper tub filled with steaming water. A beautiful cream dress was laid out on the bed. Jordie perked an eyebrow at it. The dress was indeed lovely but far too nice to wear all the time.

286

Jordie turned to Ehlowen. "This isn't a very functional outfit," she remarked.

"Functional?" Hester asked, hiding her laugh behind a cough.

"Aye, you can't do much in it because it's too pretty. How am I supposed to help the people of the clan in that?"

Ehlowen smothered the grin on her face. Hester had trouble not laughing. Meanwhile, Jordie just waited for her answer.

"Wear the dress, Jordie. Don't hurt the clan's feelings by not wearing the gown they helped prepare for you," Ehlowen said.

"Aye," Hester said. "Now I have to go see how the cookery is coming along. Wear the dress, Jordie. You'll make the clan and Locryn so proud."

Jordie gawked at them.

Something is going on and I just know it, she said to herself, crossing her arms over her chest. *If only I could figure out what it all means. I am already married to Locryn and the clan accepted me yesterday. I think. So, there is no need for all of this. But I also cannot be disrespectful to them all either. Ugh. I have to wear the beautiful but utterly useless dress.*

Sighing, she undressed. Then she sank into the copper tub to scrub off the dirt and odors of the day. Her sister-in-law picked up a washcloth and washed her back and hair.

"You don't have to help," Jordie insisted.

Ehlowen dunked her head under water and smiled when she came back up. "You know I adore your independent spirit and ample capabilities, but," she said, pouring water over Jordie's head, "you're not alone anymore. And I will tell on you to Locryn if you don't let me help."

Jordie splashed her sister with water before stepping out of the tub. Jordie threw a clean linen towel over her hair, wrapping it up to help dry it off.

As Hester mentioned, she didn't want to insult the clan by not wearing it. Ehlowen put a soft shift over her head. Ehlowen helped her lace and tie the back to the cream-colored, beaded, lacey, frilly dress she had to wear for the evening meal.

After she was dressed, Ehlowen brushed and braided her hair into a halo, her nimble fingers flickering over her head, twisting it and tucking in flowers as she went. When her sister-in-law was finished, Jordie's hair was a masterpiece.

Jordie looked in the mirror over on the wall next to her wardrobe. The greens, pinks, and yellows of the flowers looked bright against the red of her hair. Then with the cream of her dress and the tanned color of her skin, she looked to be glimmering in gold.

Jordie stared at her reflection and smiled.

Ehlowen clapped her hands. "Now you are ready!"

"I am so hungry," Jordie said.

"Well, let's go then."

Arm in arm, the two sisters descended the stairs, making their way to the doors of the castle.

JORDIE IN CHARGE

CHAPTER THIRTY-TWO

The double doors of the castle opened with a burst of bright yellow light. Jordie, with her gorgeous golden-brown eyes, gazed around the vast dining hall, looking for him. But he knew that she wouldn't be able to see him from where he was hiding. She looked absolutely stunning. She literally made it difficult for him to catch his breath. He was surprised to see that she was wearing the same beautiful dress Ehlowen wore to her own wedding.

He could see her walking around the tables in a confused manner. She delicately touched the winter holly that was picked this morning while she was with Ehlowen—but she didn't know any of this. Or anything that was going on, because it was all for her. She walked around another table before Ehlowen pulled her down the corridor to the left into Thomas's study.

Locryn came out of his hiding place, smirking as he heard her complain about how hungry she was. Ehlowen could be heard reassuring her that the food was on its way.

"Da!" Boden came bounding up to him. "She doesn't know! She doesn't have a clue!"

"Aye, and that be wonderful, son," Locryn replied, hugging his boy. "D'ye think she will like this surprise?"

Boden tapped a finger to his chin. "Aye, she will like it. Mum never had a surprise before. Shall I go get her now?"

"Aye, but keep her busy fer a few moments longer, all right?"

Boden took off down the corridor while Locryn made his way to the kitchens to see if everything else was ready to go out all at once. The cooks were bustling all over the place, putting the finishing touches on all the dishes. He walked outside to see his smiling clan standing outside the big double doors, dressed in their best and ready to see their laird's wife.

Locryn smiled, clapping his hands together and returning to the dining hall. His people came bustling in. Mothers merrily set their children down on the benches while the men brought in the alter with herbs tied to it.

He walked around, chatting and smiling with everyone. His son was doing a great job at keeping his mother busy. Eiffel, Hester, and the other kitchen cooks carried out heaping plates of food, setting it all down on the nicely dressed tables with the good plates they used for celebrating.

"Thank ye, everyone, fer helpin' me make this day special fer me wife." Locryn stood on a chair and said to his people, "She ne'er had somethin' special, somethin' good, but this night be a night she will remember, and fer that I have ye all ta thank."

"Go get the lass," Finn yelled.

"Aye, I will. Knowin' her, she be right hungry by now."

Sure enough, he could hear his wife grumble from down the hallway as the door opened. The clan got quiet, waiting to see her. The priest got into position at the front of the high table, smiling. Locryn stood off to the left of the priest and waited for his wife.

"Boden, I love you very much, but I am hungry and I am sure you are too, so let's see if we can eat yet," he could hear her say.

"But Mum, want to see my new trick? I know you're hungry, but wait a minute. Mum, Mum, Mum, wait, Mum, watch this, Mum!" Boden tried his best to hold his mother back for a few moments longer.

"Jordie, put this on real fast," Ehlowen said.

"There be a surprise fer ye," Thomas added, "so ye'll just have ta trust us."

"All right," Locryn heard her grumble, "lead the way, laird."

Locryn was chuckling as she rounded the corner and came into view. She looked absolutely radiant in the dress. Her hair was done up with lace and winter flowers intertwined. Her skin glowed, as the sleeves were short and the neckline was low, revealing the tops of her perky sun-kissed breasts.

Despite her blindfold, she smiled as she walked down the rows of benches towards him. Thomas led her by the elbow to where he was. Locryn couldn't keep the smile from his face.

"Ready, Jordie?" Thomas asked approaching his brother.

Jordie nodded. "Is it scary?"

"Terrifyin'," he said, passing Jordie off to his brother.

"Then I don't want to look."

"Verra funny, Thomas," Locryn said, scowling.

"What is going on?" she asked.

Locryn took her hands in his. "Why, Jordie, I be given ye somethin' proper."

She didn't find his tone of voice amusing. "What?" Jordie asked. "What is going on? Something is happening behind my back and I don't like it."

"Wife, it be goin' on in front o' yer face, no' behind yer back."

Jordie licked her lips. "Can I take the blindfold off yet?"

He came around behind her and placed a kiss on her neck. Then he untied the blindfold, careful of her beautifully done hair.

•••••

Jordie waited for him to remove the blindfold so she could see. But instead, he was kissing her, causing her to become unsteady. She knew he was grinning behind her. Then the blindfold fell away. Jordie scrunched her face and blinked a few times. When her eyes adjusted to the light, her mouth dropped open.

Boden stood beside Locryn, grinning from ear to ear. The dining hall was lit with stately candles. Holly and winter evergreen wreaths graced the tables, sending their perfume into the air. Everyone wore a smile, clapping and hollering for her and Locryn.

Jordie twirled in a circle, tears brimming in her eyes. She hid behind her hands, smiling and crying at the love and generosity of not only Locryn but her clan as well. She wiped the tears from her eyes, looking at Locryn with loving adoration.

"Thank you," she said, grabbing his hands.

Locryn cupped her face. "Och, Jordie," he said, kissing her, "yer the best thing that ever came inta me life. Yer me soul," he kissed her again, "fer Corwaithe brought us together. And I will love ye ferever."

She kissed him ardently back. "And I will love you forever longer."

"Verra good," Thomas said with a smile, holding up a mug of ale in a toast, "because the priest be right here ta make it ferever fer a second time."

"Forever again," Jordie said, beaming at her husband.

"Aye, ferevermore." Locryn planted a kiss on her luscious lips.

JORDIE IN CHARGE

EPILOGUE

Year of Corwaithe—Winter 1231

Corwaithe had truly blessed her life. This time around, she had her wonderful husband by her side. Even though it was hard to let go of her control, she had to admit it felt pretty good to be waited on sometimes.

At first, they seemed to fight like deranged wapako over silly matters. Like when she would go out hunting, he wanted her to have an escort while she only wanted breathing room for a few moments. They both finally agreed on her allowing a hunter to attend her, but at a distance. Even that compromise was aggravating, but once she stepped in the forest, it was like the bodyguard didn't exist.

But now, it seemed Locryn tried to keep her pinned down more, especially after she told him he was a father. She told him at the end of springtime. After that, it seemed he had trouble letting her out of his sight, even to bathe in the bathhouse. It drove her to the brink of insanity. She could not find a moment's peace without him ogling over her shoulder to see if she was all right. Or if she was "o'er doin' it in her state," when she wasn't big at all.

Thank goodness for her dear friends. If it wasn't for Ehlowen and Hester, she didn't know what she would do. Too many times, she felt like grabbing a club to whack her husband over the head, just to get him to calm down. She even tried using the baby as an excuse, telling him that he was stressing the child. But it didn't work. Locryn would come back and say, "Ye only be stressed, wife, because ye have a wee bairn growing' in yer belly. Go lie down befer ye pass oot."

Hearing those few words every damn day made her want to pull her hair out. She threatened to kill him on the spot if he did not leave her alone for ten minutes. The baby was fine, but it was his constant, ever-frustrating presence that bothered her. And thankfully that is where Ehlowen and Hester stepped in.

Clever Ehlowen got Locryn out of the room their shared by sending him on a mission to make pieces of furniture "for the bairn." Ehlowen left, hot on Locryn's heels, ticking off items that the baby "absolutely must have." Hester packed Jordie a light basket of food and together the women went for an outing in the forest, bodyguard in tow.

Once her husband was out of sight, Jordie and Hester made a break for the forest. Jordie waddled right along to her other favorite secret spot. Hester had trouble keeping up, but eventually they both made it to a little rock pool hidden behind several fallen trees. Jordie climbed over the trees with ease and sat on a log, looking down at the rock pool.

"And you had to eat a meal here?" Hester asked, huffing and puffing.

"Well, it is very beautiful, is it not?"

"Aye, it's pretty, but it's quite some ways from the keep."

"It's not that far," Jordie said, seeing the very edge of the castle wall from the log. "I only need a few minutes of sitting here, breathing in the fresh air. Now I can actually hear myself think. For once."

Hester laughed. "That man loves you, that is for certain. I have never seen a man act so towards his pregnant wife."

"I love him more than I can say, but sometimes I feel like I cannot go pee without his consent or him being *right* there," Jordie said.

"And I will always be *right* there," Locryn said coming up to her. He crossed his arms and scowled.

Jordie sighed. At least she'd had a nice long walk in the forest by herself and gotten to sit there for a few moments.

"I love you, Locryn, but I need a moment to myself once in a while."

"Aye and ye can have a moment ta yerself, wife—in the West Tower, in our chamber."

"I need fresh air."

"Breathe oot the window."

"But I want to walk around."

"Ye can walk yerself back ta our chamber."

Jordie didn't know whether she felt more defeated, angry, or irritated. But it all was coming to a boiling point. One word more and she would either knock him out or cry. The babe was due anytime, and with each passing day, Locryn grew more controlling.

"You are the most annoying person I have ever known!"

"And ye, Jordie, dinna listen verra well."

"Don't listen very well."

"Dinna correct me!"

"Don't control me!"

"Wife," he growled.

Jordie smirked, "Husband."

"Get yer wee waddlin' arse back ta our chamber."

"Why are you so abyss-bent on keeping me secluded at home? Why? What have I done?" She started to cry. "I just wanted to walk and smell the air in the forest since you took hunting away from me, and now you want to take breathing and walking away from me too."

●●●●●

Locryn was exasperated. Jordie questioned him at every turn and did the exact opposite of what he asked her to. She mistook his caring and concern for her and their babe as control. He wasn't trying to control her, he was trying to help since she was so sick the majority of the pregnancy.

"Sweetlin'," Locryn began as patiently as he could, "I only want ta take care o' ye, surely ye ken that."

Jordie sniffed, "Aye, I do."

Locryn came up to the top part of the log, pulling her close against his body. "Then, wee love, let me take care o' ye as a man should."

Jordie wiped her eyes. "Will you let me walk back to the keep?"

Locryn closed his eyes, trying not to become more frustrated. "If ye promise ta rest after."

She smiled brightly at him. "I do so promise."

Hester snickered behind them. Locryn shot her a quieting glance. Hester picked up the basket of food and headed back to the castle with the bodyguard.

Locryn helped his wife down off the rest of the fallen trees. Even though she was big, she was nimble and strong. She was always up to mischief, trying to keep doing things she had always done.

Last week he caught her at the smithy sharpening the arrow heads for her bow. And the week before that, he caught her in the butcher's shop, skinning the dead animals Nirran killed. Aye, his wee wife was always up to something. She wouldn't slow down and put her feet up for more than five minutes. But he had a remedy for that now.

A smile tugged his lips. Once they got back to the keep and got her up in their chamber to rest, he was going to lock her in there for the whole day. She was going to relax—whether she liked it or not.

"I need to stop for a second," she puffed.

"Be ye all right?" he asked, placing a hand over her back.

"Aye, I am fine."

Hester came back to see what was taking them so long. "The babe has dropped. She'll be coming soon," she said, smiling. "She is a bit early though, I think."

"How do you know it's a she?" Jordie asked.

"I just know," Hester replied. "When you've seen as many bairns be born as I—"

"We need ta get ye home, wife," Locryn interrupted. "This be no place for a babe ta be born."

Jordie rolled her eyes. "She isn't coming yet. I would be feeling it and then my water would break."

"Ye dinna ken that," he countered.

"Aye, I do. I had a son before this, Locryn. Moreover, I know what happens with my body better than you do."

Locryn frowned, putting his hands on his hips. "Dinna fight me on this. We need ta get ye back ta the keep."

"I am not fighting you, Locryn. I'm merely telling you what happens first."

"Jordie," Locryn grumbled, "do I need ta carry ye?"

"No," Jordie said straightening up, proving she was fine. "Let's go."

●●●●●

They walked for a bit more before Locryn decided that she walked enough and carried her. He remarked on how swollen her feet were in those slippers and how low the baby had dropped. The whole time she said nothing. It was a waste of breath to share her experience with childbearing since he had already stopped listening.

Once they passed under the black iron gates, Locryn started barking orders for someone to get the midwife. Jordie yelled back that the babe wasn't coming yet and to ignore her husband's foolish screaming. Locryn shifted her in his arms and covered her mouth with his hand. He couldn't do both and had to set her down.

The clans people they passed roared with laughter. Locryn eventually set her down in the castle yard. Jordie immediately used Hester as a shield between her and her husband, hollering over Hester's shoulder that she was just fine and he needed to settle down. Locryn tried to grab hold of her but she was too quick in pulling Hester in front of her. Before long, she was laughing at her frustrated husband.

"Care to listen to me now?" she giggled.

"Yer too much trouble, wife."

"Aye, well, you knew that before you married me," she laughed. "The babe isn't coming for a while yet, so calm your crazy, ever-loving mind."

"Dinna scold me in front o' me own clan," Locryn got serious.

"I be no' scoldin'," Jordie countered.

Locryn covered his face with his hands, wiping his face in irritation. "Wife," he began.

"Husband."

"Ye will do what I say."

"You have to catch me first!" She took off running towards the West Tower.

The clan was watching, laughing behind her as she ran quite swiftly though pregnant.

Jordie laughed and laughed as she ran, going up the stairs. She knew Locryn was right behind her, but she was going to win. She took the stairs two at a time, reaching the door to their chamber first.

As she thought, her husband was right behind her. He slammed the door behind him, striding forward to her with a seriousness that she had never seen before.

She gazed at him, confused. "Aye?"

"Lay down, wife," he commanded, gently pushing her back towards the bed.

•••••

He unbuttoned her trews that she still insisted on wearing even though he knew she would be much more comfortable in the dress he'd had made for her. He pulled them off and threw them over his shoulder. Next, he went around to the side of the bed where she had her stash of weaponry—her bow, arrows, hatchet and a few knives—and took them all, going back out the door and setting them down on the step.

"Lay," he barked at her.

Jordie laid back down, watching him, waiting. He unbuttoned his trews, kicked them off and straddled her, pinning her arms down. Her eyes were heavy with want and desire for him to love her hard and long. He couldn't say no to those twinkling eyes of hers.

Locryn helped to flip her over to her hands and knees as he didn't want to crush the babe as he entered her. It didn't take her long to come and her moans of ecstasy undid him just as quickly. He kept driving into her for a while until she came at least a few times more, wanting her to be so satisfied that she had no choice but to rest. It was highly enjoyable but he was trying to win a war with his wife. He knew that if he loved her for a while longer, make her come a few more times, that she would become so tired and rest for a few hours.

His plan worked.

To his relief, after she cleaned herself off a bit from their joyous lovemaking, she fell asleep in the chair next to the fireplace. He kissed her lovingly on the forehead and left the chamber.

He locked the door quietly, not wanting to wake his adventurous wife. She needed to rest and sleep before the babe came. If Hester was right, the babe would be coming soon. He needed to make sure that her room was ready and that the midwife was ready as well.

Locryn walked back down the stairs to the middle chamber. This room became his pet project when she first told him that she was with child right after the Spring Feast. That was the best night of his life, getting told that he was soon to be a father.

He checked then double-checked the room, making certain there were enough cloths for the babe and her or his wee bottom. He hoped he was going to be having a girl for he was lucky enough to already have a smart, talented son.

"Da!" Boden poked his head in the room. "Is Mum going to be having the babe soon?" he asked excitedly.

His son had grown a few inches and packed on a few pounds since he had first arrived. He had the making of a true leader. The other children loved the friendly boy and the adults respected him. He learned warrior skills and other manly tasks quickly but was humble enough to admit his mistakes and to ask questions as to what was wrong or could be improved upon. Aye, Locryn was a proud father, made that way by his wonderful son.

"Yer stubborn mum doesna think so."

"I hope it's a girl. I would like to have a wee sister."

Locryn gave his son a hug. "I hope so too."

"What are you going to name her?"

"I want ta name her Madigan, Maddie fer short, but yer mum wants ta name her Miera."

"I like Madigan—it sounds fierce."

"Aye, a fierce little dog, like yer wee mum. Dinna tell her I said that."

Boden burst out laughing. "Aye! Mum is like a dog, always barkin'."

Locryn hushed his son. "Dinna let yer mum hear that. I swear, her bein' with child has improved her hearin', among other things."

"Just in case, can we get some sugar buns to make her happy?" Boden asked. "Food always makes her easier to, umm, to deal with?"

Locryn laughed.

Ever since Locryn got his son his first taste of a sugared bun, the lad could not seem to get enough of them. And his mother never let Locryn forget that it was all his fault their son was addicted to them.

"Aye. But dinna tell yer mum."

●●●●●

She woke up with severe back pain, arrowhead sharp and shooting down her leg. Jordie rose stiffly to her feet and stretched herself out, only to find that the back pain wasn't her only concern. She was in labor.

She must have been so tired that she slept through what her body was preparing for her to do. Still, she was thankful for the rest that she had been too stubborn to admit she needed. And also for the loving that her husband gave her many times over. If this babe was anything like Boden, it would be coming fast.

When she made her way to the door to call down the stairs, she stumbled, rolling her ankle as she caught herself from falling. She cursed but got right back up. Where was that husband of hers? He should be here, bugging her to sleep more or to eat something.

"Locryn," she cried out.

No answer returned.

Jordie got to her feet, limping to the door. Finally, she made it and leaned against the door for support, calling for help.

Silence.

Jordie tried the door and found it locked.

That sneaky man!

Frustrated, she called out again, only to receive silence as her answer. Waddling and limping, she made her way over to the window. She had to pause as a contraction overtook her body. It sent waves of racking clenches in her stomach. Her insides felt like a wet towel being wrung out of water as hard as possible, then twisted more than the fabric could handle. But Jordie was defiant. She would force her way out of this damned chamber he had stupidly locked her in.

The window was wide open, thankfully. So, she stuck her head out, looking to see if she could spot anyone outside. To her utter amazement, no one was there.

"Locryn?" she called again.

She scowled.

"Locryn!" she yelled louder. "Damn you, you bloody eejit—*Locryn!*"

"Aye, Jordie?" Finn's head poked out from around the corner.

Relief flooded her senses. But another contraction seized her and it must have shown.

"Milady!" Finn yelled up, "be ye all right? Be the bairn comin'?"

"Please get my idiot husband who locked me up in here."

Finn laughed, "He locked ye in there?"

"Aye, the blasted man!"

Finn laughed so hard he keeled over. "That braw man. I canna wait ta see what ye will do ta him when he gets up there."

Frustrated, Jordie said, "First I need to have this baby, then I am going to smack him for locking me in here, and last I am going to—" another stronger contraction came and she yelped, "—I'm going to smack you if you don't hurry it up."

Finn looked surprised. "The bairn truly be comin', lass?"

"Yes, for bloody sake, yes!" she yelled. "Bloody men and their double-checking idiocy!"

Finn took off like a hound on a scent to find her husband.

Gordon stood by, yelling at her to breathe and letting her know that Finn would be right back, before he too hurried away.

"Stupid men!" she cursed aloud.

She left the window and went to the end of their bed. She clung to the bed railing as fluid from inside her body gushed out all over the wooden floor. Her water broke. It seemed like forever and Locryn still wasn't here. She needed him. She didn't want to be alone as she brought another life into this world.

"Where are you?" she cried out as she pushed.

•••••

Locryn and Boden waited in the kitchen for Kealey to pull the buns out of the oven and glaze them. The pungent steam wafted and circled around their noses. His son literally drooled.

"Wipe your face, lad," Locryn said.

Kealey handed Boden the first sweet bun, which the lad promptly devoured. Locryn was about to take a bite

310

when Ehlowen, Thomas, Marcy, and Gordon flew into the kitchens with smiles on their faces. Confused, Locryn looked at them all, staring at him.

He perked a curious eyebrow.

"Aye?" he asked.

"And why ye no' be with yer wee wife?" Thomas questioned.

"Aye," Finn teased, "I thought ye canna get enough o' the troublesome woman?"

"Aye, well, the trouble be sleepin' like she should be," Locryn retorted and scowled.

"Ye sure she be sleepin', milaird?" Finn asked.

"Dinna ken, Finn," Thomas replied. "I thought she be awake and yellin'."

Locryn stood with his hands on his hips.

"Aye," Finn said, "I was sure she be wide awake yellin' fer ye because the bairn be comin'."

Locryn's face went pale and he flew out of the room as if an angry wapako snapped at his heels. He rounded the corner to the West Tower and heard his wife screaming for him. The midwife was talking to his wife through the door. When Elyria saw him, she scowled and shook her gray head. His fingers trembled on the keys as he unlocked the door, only to find her sweating and trembling. She was down on her knees, her hips spread wide as she clutched the bedframe for dear life.

He ran over to his wife, trying to scoop her up and put her in bed, but she swatted him away.

"You're an idiot," she scowled at him as he pushed her hair out of her face. "Why would you lock the damn door?"

Concerned, he rubbed her back. "I wanted ye ta rest, lass."

Jordie snorted derisively.

"Be ye all right, Jordie?" Marcy called from the doorway.

Jordie smiled at his sister.

He was glad she was here and came around to his wonderful wife. At first Marcy and Jordie didn't like each other. Then one night they brawled at a feast, leaving a bloody, bruised mess in their wake. After that, they were best friends, hardly inseparable at times. He never once understood it but he was grateful at least another one of his family came around.

Bellamy passed away in spring, just after Jordie announced she was pregnant. His mother was still not fond of Jordie, but she was excited to be a grandmother again.

"I am fine, Marcy. Thanks for coming," she said, smiling weakly.

"Wouldn't miss it." Marcy came over and sat on the bed, massaging Jordie's arms.

Ehlowen, who couldn't handle other people's bodily functions, left the room but yelled back encouragement and love. Thomas nodded at him, following his wife out. Jordie quaked and gritted her teeth, clutching the bed frame.

"Ye all right, love?" Locryn asked.

"Aye, I am fine. I just have a little being trying to come out of a hole the size of an orange," she yelled, white-knuckling the bed frame and huffing.

The midwife murmured encouragement in between the contractions. Jordie let out another long groan, trying to push their babe out of her small body. She hung her sweaty head in exhaustion. Marcy still sat on the bed rubbing her arms, telling her not to rush it, that the babe would come in due time. Locryn could tell that his wife was growing irritated, so he motioned for Marcy to hush.

Instead, Jordie and Marcy conversed here and there. Thomas had a man bring up the copper bathtub while the midwife prepped it with luke-warm water and herbs. Locryn felt utterly useless. He got up to leave once, but the look on Jordie's bonny face, called him back. She needed him here whether he was helpful or not.

Locryn kissed her head and he sat in the chair for a while, hoping that the bath would make her quickly tiring body relax. She climbed into the tub, trying her absolute best to enjoy the water but after a short few moments, she got out, going back to the bed, this time standing.

His poor wee wife looked positively exhausted yet she still labored on for over an hour. She refused the soak again in the bathtub. She was dripping in sweat, her long shift wet with sweat as she stood at the end of their bed.

He was able to get her to sit on the edge of the bed for a bit while he rubbed her back and massaged her. The minute another contraction hit, she stood and pushed as hard as her body would allow.

"This bairn be a stubborn wee lass," the midwife Elyria said.

"Aye, she be stubborn just like her wee mum," Marcy teased.

Jordie smirked, "Nay, more like her father."

"I be no' stubborn," he countered.

"Aye, you're not stubborn. Like the sun doesn't rise in the east."

Marcy snickered.

"I be no' stubborn," he repeated.

Jordie smirked. "You locked me in our chamber."

He had nothing to say to that. Somehow, she could tell what he was thinking because she was smiling at him.

"By the Goddess, this child is stubborn too," Jordie gritted out as a contraction shook her body.

"The bairn be right there, Jordie," the midwife said. "Just a few more pushes now."

As another contraction came, he could tell his wife was preparing for the long shot, as she planted her heels and bore down. She yelped once as she squeezed the railing for support.

A squeal pierced the air as their babe came into the world.

Locryn caught Jordie right before she collapsed to the floor and Elyria caught the newly born child. He went to the ground with her, grasping her in his powerful arms. She leaned her tired head against him as he kissed the side of her head. Elyria cleaned off the crying babe, handing the child to her mother.

Tears flooded her eyes. "Oh, Locryn," she cried. "Our little girl is so beautiful."

"She be perfect, just like her mum," Locryn said through his own warm tears. "I love ye, Jordie, so verra much."

"And I love you," she said. "She is so lovely!"

"Aye, our wee Madigan." He kissed his baby girl.

"Aye, little Maddie."

The babe squealed and cried.

"I think ye likes yer name," Locryn cooed to his daughter. "Little Maddie." His fingers brushed her small hand. "Ye will be fierce like yer mum."

"She already is." Jordie kissed her head.

"And she will be controllin' as well," he teased his wife.

"Don't call me controlling."

"Aye, ye be," Marcy added, "Jordie in charge!"

"Jordie in control," Locryn chuckled.

"Madigan will be every bit like me if you keep it up!"

"All right, wife, let's get ye inta bed so ye can rest."

Locryn helped her off the floor while Marcy pulled back the sheets on the bed. Jordie got in with Maddie asleep on her chest. Locryn laid down beside her, his right arm wrapped around her. Jordie asked Marcy to go find their son, so he could meet Madigan.

Marcy went to the door, opening it to find Boden sitting on the steps, patiently waiting to see his baby sister.

Boden came in with a smile. He came around to the right side of the bed, where his already present grin got wider.

"Mum," Boden said, "she is so tiny." Boden reached out with a timid finger, touching Madigan on the head. "I love her!"

Maddie was long, with tiny hands, long fingers, and a mop of blonde hair like her father's. It was too early to tell what color eyes she would have, but already Jordie could tell their little babe would be stubborn like herself with the handsome features of her father.

Marcy ushered Boden out of the room so she could rest. Jordie told him that she would be up and around within a few hours, but she just needed a nap.

Boden left, talking animatedly to Marcy about all that he wanted to do with Maddie when she got older and wasn't so small.

Jordie smiled, then stifled a yawn.

"Jordie in charge," she murmured as she slipped into sleep. "I am not that controlling."

Locryn kissed her head and snorted. "Stubborn wife."

ABOUT THE AUTHOR

In the land of JRR Tolkien, Ericka would be a hobbit; hairy, small and lover of feasts. Barely reaching over five feet tall, the stay at home mother of two writes at her small, unimpressive desk daily to deliver a tale delved from her past.

Her small, sausage fingers scribble unintelligible words that are thankfully fixed by her word processor. She hoards toys in bins. She ravenously eats meals her kids overlook, and she lovingly washes the garments worn by her hard-working, supportive husband.

Ericka works diligently on her novels to give compelling pieces of literature that would have otherwise filled a dwarf's vast diamond mine, instead of bookshelves at the local stores. Being only 27 years of age, this hobbit still has a lot of adventure to fulfill before she settles down to second breakfast.

Ericka hopes you enjoy her books. She hopes adventure finds you, grabs hold, and drags you out of your front yard, you little Bilbo!

ACKNOWLEDGEMENTS

I want to thank my publisher, Teresa McPherson, for believing in me, and encouraging me to write more, to make it different and better than the last. You are truly a lovely person and I am honored to get to know someone as brilliant and wonderful as you.

I also want to thank my editor, Lauren Moore, for giving me the loving yet positive constructive criticism that I needed for this book and all the others to truly stand out and be amazing. You are truly a rare gem. I am grateful not only for your edits but also for your friendship.

Thank you, fellow writer of another genre, J. R. Handley, for your direction, friendship and assistance.

Thank you, T. M. Toombs, fellow writer of another amazing genre for your advice, friendship and encouraging assistance.

Lastly, thank you, to my best friend and the love of my life, Bryan. Your believing in me, made this all possible. Your standing beside me is more than I will ever be able to describe. I love you honey. This first book is for you.

AVALEE'S VOICE

COMING IN DECEMBER 2017

Avalee stood on the rocky crags overlooking the Wandering Sea. She anguished over the plague decimating her people. A third of the population have died in less than a fortnight. And Avalee was determined to save them.

King Folerman, King of Swanshé, presented Avalee with an opportunity to do just that - marry a Meerdoran Laird's son and receive provisions and medicaments in return. Avalee agreed.

Unbeknownst to Avalee, her new husband, Justin, was forced into this marriage, unlike her. The Laird, Kent Hernan, had decided Avalee is what Justin needs, as well as being an asset to the clan. A master carpenter is always welcome.

Avalee finds herself in a new land married to a man that loathes her and his brother who is not her fan either.

Will Corwaithe save her?
   Will Avalee find her voice?

319

CALIDA'S FORGE

COMING IN 2018

From dawn until dusk, Calida's hammer stuck the hot metal on her anvil. Calida shaped it, molded it, and produced the finest quality weapons in all of Swanshé. The entirety of her existence was all for her sister, Cora.

Seeking a new opportunity away from the prejudice of their town, Calida and Cora left Swanshé for the land of Meerdora where dreams supposedly came true. Calida searched for a better living – both in her work and among her new neighbors.

Settling into the small town of Palasida, located a half days ride from the castle of Rowanoake, Calida set up her new forge. Business was booming. Neighbors were great. Cora made friends. Life was grand.

Devastated by the loss of Cora, Calida spirals into darkness. In her grief, Calida finds solace in her forge, that is, until an old evil comes sauntering back into Calida's life, seeking to destroy her very being.

Will Calida save herself from this evil or will she be rescued?

63883341R00182

Made in the USA
San Bernardino, CA
20 December 2017